To Taylie —
You are the first
Love + Blessings —
Mani

Soul's Sojourn

An autobiographical fiction

by Mani Pureheart

Published by F.O.T.L. Press

Bend, Oregon

ManiPureheart.com

Cover Design by Mani Pureheart

ISBN: 979-8-9869243-1-1

Printed in the U.S.A.

ACKNOWLEDGMENTS

First and foremost, to my beloved wife and partner of 34 years, Kim, who has ridden this sometimes-turbulent creative wave with me. She has been my chief navigator, inspiration, hand-holder, and, when needed, the gadfly that kept me on course and made sure that I kept the words flowing onto the screen. THANK YOU!

To Risa Scranton, nitpicker extraordinaire!

To Adrienne Young, who asked all the right questions, and facilitated a far deeper connection with my life and times as Davol loch Namor than I would have achieved on my own.

To Jodi Jones and Alesha Jess, for playing along with an old man's fantasy…or is it?

And to Hope Eksten, Keith Turner, Joshua Kamp, Valerie Spencer, Carl Miller, et al., for believing in, and inspiring me to go far beyond my comfort zone.

It's a long list, but I also want to thank Karen Larsen, Chelsea Monter, Yvonne Sloan, Drinda Bell, Wendy White, Cherie Smith, Debra Fant, Angie Romero, Donna Eden, Chuck Allen, and all the others who have offered encouragement, feedback, love, and support for my personal sojourn.

Dedicated to Ada

You ARE the magic!
Go forth, now,

and

CHANGE THE WORLD!

and to

Kim

… I'd love another dance with you …

…and Toibl, Tattie and Robo…

TABLE OF CONTENTS

BOOK ONE—IN THE BEGINNING…

BOOK TWO—TRAVELERS…

BOOK THREE—THE JOURNEY CONTINUES

SOUL'S SOJOURN

A fictionalized account of an ongoing true story that may or may not
have ever occurred.

BOOK ONE—IN THE BEGINNING…

"IN A TRULY INFINITE REALITY, NOT ONLY IS EVERYTHING IMAGINABLE POSSIBLE, IT HAS ALREADY HAPPENED AN INFINITE NUMBER OF TIMES."
(Mani Pureheart)

And it came to pass, in the 187th year of his youth, as decreed and prophesied by The Namor, that Agon, 112th descendant of Namor, Son of the Stars, of the House of Namor, and his beloved partner Eedor, conceived the male child, who was to be the last of line Namor on Earth.

And his name was given to be Davol;

Davol loch Namor.

In his twelfth year, Davol was sent to the stars for thirty-five Earth-years, to study among his kin and others of the star peoples, the many lessons that were to be his tools for the next eight-plus centuries of his existence in that body upon the planet called Earth.

These are stories from that life and others.

CHAPTER 1—Every Ending is a Beginning in Disguise

Firefinger hunkered down next to the splintered, mossy stump in the twilight damp at the edge of the deep forest. A light rain was falling, more like a heavy mist. His dark, forest-green cloak was wrapped loosely around him, disguising his form as he squatted there. The voluminous hood, redolent of a thousand campfires, covered his head and caressed his cheeks with shadow, hiding his piercing eyes.

He watched intently across the short distance of moonlit meadow as his funeral pyre burned fiercely in the night. Those who had captured and killed him caroused and danced long into the night with copious drinking, ribald song, and loud boasts of bravery thrown carelessly to the wind. The capricious shafts of moonlight filtering through the feathery, rapidly moving clouds, gave glimpses of faces drunk and distorted with wine and blood-lust. The roaring fire backlit the gyrating, staccato figures of the revelers dancing to the music of the crackling flames. His impaled head, still dripping his life's blood, grinned maniacally at him from atop the crude pole his captors had stuck into the loamy ground. It would soon be painted with pitch and displayed as a great prize at the Dark One's castle keep.

Firefinger was a man of the woods, a shadowy forest figure in a worn huntsman's cloak. Coming from nowhere, found wherever and whenever he wished. A confident man. His confidence showed in every footstep; in the way he carried himself. He had come from good stock, with Star blood running in his veins thanks to a many-times great grandparent. His father, Conrad, had been an expert woodsman and hunter, skilled in surviving in the outdoors, and, in his homeland, a high priest of the Ancient Ones, a magician, and an adventurer who was driven from his homeland, then, much later, killed by his enemies.

Conrad had fled across the great water into a new country and new adventures with his wife and infant son. He had trained Firefinger from a very early age in every woodsman's skill and the use of his natural magical skills and abilities. Firefinger's Druid mother had taught him herbal medicine and the secrets of its preparations and uses. Through his father's lineage, the family also had a very strong streak of psychic, energetic abilities and sensitivities, in which Conrad was careful to train his son thoroughly.

Firefinger's bronzed body was as sturdy as an Oak, and he stood a half head taller than most of the general population. His ruggedly handsome face was framed by dark brown hair pulled back into a shoulder-length ponytail and a short beard that came to a blunt point just below his chin. He sported a small but noticeable star-shaped scar in the middle of his forehead, just over his third eye, from a childhood encounter with a black walnut tree stump. He had been out with his parents collecting the nuts and some herbs when he tripped on a root and struck his head on the stump. The stump won the battle, leaving him with the first of the many scars, which would mark his body and tell the tale of his life.

Turning soundlessly at last from the grisly scene, Firefinger began to make his way through the semi-darkness of the deep forest night. He was skilled and experienced, comfortable and capable in the forest. The ground beneath his feet seemed to welcome his steps. It was springy, silent, and soft. No sound betrayed him as his careful feet habitually found the safest place, without twigs or loose leaves that might reveal his passage. As he passed, the thick layer underfoot gave off the unmistakably pungent, rich fragrance of vibrant life hidden beneath. Small creatures of the night rustled away as they moved through the fallen leaves. Walking silently and judiciously, as was his nature, he took well over an hour to carefully make his way back under the shrouded moon to the haven of his carefully hidden camp where the child, whom he had named Chedrick, lay sleeping.

An owl hooted in the distance.

Firefinger smiled.

CHAPTER 2—Chedrick

Nearly eleven years before, while traveling in a remote area known to have roving bands of marauders, Firefinger had come across the smoldering remains of a barn.

That rustic home had been the abode of Medore, and his wife, Emma the Lame. They had lived there for five years, building a future from the abundant land.

Three years before, the sweet autumn clematis, which clung to the south side of their humble home, had been in full bloom, and the fragrance was intoxicating. As she sat there spinning, watching, and daydreaming, Emma became aware of a raven watching her from a branch of a small tree only a few feet away. Ravens were common in Derf, and on their farm, but it was most unusual for one to stay so close. Assured that she had finally noticed him, the bird hopped a couple of steps closer to her on the branch, never breaking eye contact. Emma saw a dangling red string holding a clay pendant, hanging from its beak.

Keeping eye contact, the raven finally hopped from the tip of the branch it had been sitting on, and onto the top of her spinning wheel. With a barely-heard squawk, the bird dropped the pendant from his beak into her lap and flew off. The curious object tumbled out of the folds of her dress and onto the earth below. She did not see the raven's eyes turn a bright blue for a moment, nor its plumage change fleetingly from black to snow-white as her eye was fixed on the strange amulet, now laying on the ground at her feet.

Greatly bewildered, Emma picked up the pendant and looked at its blank surface. "What is this?," she wondered. Puzzling over it and turning it round and round in her hand she finally flipped it over and saw what looked like a sketch of a heart within a circle. There seemed to be a faint, blue glow to the design, barely discernible against the off-white of the clay.

"What an odd thing," she thought, tucking it into the pocket of her apron and promptly forgetting it.

Emma the Lame was enjoying one of the last few days of warmth and had placed her spinning wheel just outside the door of their farmhouse where she could enjoy watching her husband, Medore, go about the daily chores of their small farm. A smart and beautiful girl, when she was only ten years old, she was helping her mother with the milking when a cow became startled and suddenly stepped back, breaking Emma's right leg. The leg healed poorly, and while she could walk, she did so painfully and slowly. Despite her beauty, her parents secretly wondered if she would ever find a husband. In the farmlands of Derf, a woman's role was not easy.

Her mind wandered back to other matters. It had now been two months since she had bled and her modest bosom had become sore to the touch. It seemed that she might be with child. She and Medore had been together for almost five years and had all but given up hope of ever becoming parents. She would tell Medore of her possible pregnancy, but first, she would wait a few weeks more to be sure. There had been two false starts before, and she did not want to raise her husband's hopes only to have them dashed once more.

The spinning continued as she returned to thoughts of all the permutations and repercussions a pregnancy would bring.

Six weeks later, while Medore was at the edge of the property mending a fence, he heard something light hit the ground beside his feet. At the same time, he heard a raven calling as its wings carried it off into the distance. Looking around, he found a small flat disc of clay. Picking it up, he saw an image of a heart within a circle. There was a tiny white feather that had adhered to it. He casually looked the talisman over, as men are wont to do, then nonchalantly chucked it off to the right and out of his way. He did not notice the faint blue glow of the design.

His tasks complete, the disc forgotten, and the end of the day nigh, Medore began the short walk back to their cottage, and dinner.

Emma had prepared a rich stew from the root vegetables in their garden and some venison. Dinner was quiet. Medore was tired, Emma thoughtful. Finally, she spoke, "Darling Medore, I believe I am with child. It has been almost four months since I bled and my breasts are tender and swelling."

Medore, in mid-swallow, froze and nearly choked on the piece of venison he had been eating. "What?," he demanded. "What did you say? Are you SURE?"

A huge smile blossomed slowly over his handsome, rugged face. His hair had become quite dark as he had grown into manhood, and it set off his features like a frame. "A child? Really? You're with child?"

For a man who had been so exhausted a moment before, the transformation was astonishing. Leaping up from the table so quickly that his stool skittered across the floor and into a corner, he ran around to his wife's side of the table and awkwardly embraced her, knocking her plate to the floor. He dragged her up out of her chair and began dancing a joyous dance around her with his hands on her shoulders, spinning her round and round in the process.

"A child! You're pregnant! Are you sure? Finally! A child!" Copious tears of joy rolled down cheeks that barely knew the meaning of the word tear. Emma could only smile and nod through her tears. To be able to give her beloved husband such joy was almost more than she could bear. Shock set in and Medore collapsed on the floor in even more helpless tears and hysterical joy. A giant, lopsided grin stretched from one side of his weathered and tan face to the other. "I'm going to be a father!"

As a young man, Medore was known to be an excellent woodsman and hunter. In his heart, he had always wanted a son to share and teach all of his skills and to share the joys of a woodsman's life. "May it be so," he pleaded to the faceless gods. "May it be so."

***

And it came to pass that Emma was delivered of a boy, a healthy and robust son who was delivered at home by his father. Medore had delivered many animals in his life, but to deliver his son was a miracle he had never considered a possibility. The boy was born without any complications early in the morning after a short and easy labor.

Hours later, after the bloody cleanup had been completed and his new son lay suckling from his drowsy mother's breast, Medore finally succumbed to sleep himself, lying next to his new family in the hours before daybreak.

They would enjoy almost two years of joyful family life together.

His hunter's nose awakened him first. It was almost dawn.

Startled, he leaped from his bed and tried to gather his senses about him. Bear! He smelled bear. It was strong, and it was close by! He realized how vulnerable his tiny family was at this moment.

As he looked around for his bow and knife, a large pile of fur detached itself from the floor at the foot of their bed. It stirred and rousted itself, rising to a height that threatened the low ceiling of their cottage. The bear appeared to give off a glow of soft vibrant baby blue.

Medore stood transfixed; unable to move. In his mind, he heard the bear speak with a human voice. "Your son is your son. He is not only your son but the world's. He has returned to a physical body once more with a great mission."

The bear disappeared, and Medore awakened.

He lay for a long time in contemplation and consideration of what he had just experienced and what he had heard. While magic still existed in the world, it was not common. He remembered the bit of clay dropped by the Raven with the symbol a heart within a circle. The bear had been accompanied by that same symbol.

So, he sat some more and considered what fate had brought to him.

After checking on his wife and son, he silently began preparing breakfast for her. Eventually, the smells of his cooking awakened her. Medore told Emma of the visit from the bear, of the symbol that the bear had shown him and how that same symbol had been present on the stone the raven dropped when he was working on the fence.

He spoke reluctantly and carefully at first, but the more he spoke of it, the more animated he became as he began to realize the full import of this remarkable experience.

A strange look came over Emma's face as she remembered. "Will you bring me my apron from that hook?," she asked her husband.

Puzzled, he complied and brought her the garment. She dug determinedly into the capacious pocket of the apron, sweeping her hand from side to side, past bulbs and trimmings, her garden knife, and more, in search of something. Finally, her fingers struck gold in a corner, and her eyes lit up as she plucked from the pocket the prize that she wanted to show her husband.

Emma held up the disk, with its red cord. "On the first day that I thought I was pregnant, a raven came to me and landed on my spinning wheel before dropping this into my lap. I thought it very curious at the time, but I forgot to mention it to you. Indeed, I forgot all about it until this moment."

As the two spoke of the disk, of portents and bears and ravens, Emma laid the clay disk on a small table near their son's bed. The boy saw the disk and the brightly colored cord, and, as young children will do, wanted to hold it. He was still clutching it in his hand as he went to sleep.

CHAPTER 3—End of the World

Attacking in the night, four marauders silently came to the homestead and set fire to their outbuildings. Hearing the fearful thrashing and noises of the animals, the hapless Medore rushed out to save his livestock and barn. Out of the darkness, carrying a freshly stripped and sharpened sapling, a shadowy, lurking figure stepped from behind a tree as he passed.

The leader of the marauders was tall, thick, and burly. A hairy monster of a man with a penchant for extreme violence and cruelty. He stepped swiftly and silently behind the farmer with his chosen weapon raised high.

Driven by some mysterious sixth sense of danger, and the sense of the presence of another person, Medore swiftly wheeled around to the right just as the shaft began its murderous, arcing, descent.

The farmer was quickly impaled with the makeshift shaft in the cowardly sneak attack, like a speared fish in a shallow river. The deadly arc of the freshly peeled and slippery, sharply pointed stick had been aimed directly at the farmer's heart. Instead, the thick wooden shaft pierced the right side of his upper back, pushed aside the ribs between the shoulder blade and spine, and continued on its deadly mission. It had been brought down in a hideous arc that easily passed through his body, just missing his heart but piercing his lungs, and finally, tearing through the farmer's intestines as it exited his body. The vicious pole slid through his body from the upper back to lower abdomen in a single deadly pass.

In his final moments of clarity, Medore was amazed at the sensation of being pierced through and through. Time seemed to slow to a crawl as he observed the sensations of the shaft's passage through his body. Although he knew it was his body, it was almost as though he was observing it from a casual observer's point of view. There was a moment of shock as the point first struck and penetrated him, and the odd, queasy feeling as it passed almost effortlessly through organs and muscle before exiting just below his beltline. The sense of shock was so great that it would be almost a minute before he began to be aware of the excruciating pain that would mark his last moments in that body. As he gazed in amazement and surprise at this unwanted appendage that had suddenly blossomed where no appendage should be, he collapsed on the ground in shock.

Disabled and dying, he cried out in surprise.

Knowing that he would not be able to defend himself effectively, the farmer was left by his attacker to lie in the muck where he could slowly and helplessly expire. Emma, not knowing that there had been an attack but only hearing his anxious calls, rushed out of the house towards her stricken husband.

Two marauders stepped out of the shadows as she passed and seized her roughly. One struck her with the butt of his knife, knocking her momentarily senseless. Their crude laughter rang out as they dragged her in front of her helpless, dying husband. While two of them held her upright a third roughly cut her clothing from her body, not caring that she was cut in the process. After a brief quarrel as to who would be first, the two that had held her while the third cut her clothing from her also held her to stop her struggles while their leader, then they, each in their turn, ravaged her roughly and repeatedly before her husband's helpless and dying eyes. Her attackers laughed uproariously at her struggles and cries as she was trying in vain to simultaneously fight them off and reach her stricken husband, who was helplessly watching through fading vision as his life ebbed away.

When they were done with her, the last one to use her casually slit her throat and left her, dying there on the trampled earth.

When all was done, dawn had arrived fully, and the marauders quickly ransacked the house and the property before torching the couple's cabin. The meagre spoils of the household were hastily searched and divided amongst the members before the group scattered and fled, in fear of discovery.

Two hours later, as Firefinger approached the smoldering ruin, he saw the impaled farmer lying in a pool of darkening blood, dead. There was a crude spear protruding from his lower left side. The remainder of the makeshift lance extended some two feet from his back. It held his body in a grotesque parody of a man resting on his side or in sleep. The farmer's eyes were still open. His face reflected the horror of his final visions. In front of him, only six feet away, lay the ravaged, bloodied, and broken body of his wife, Emma. Her shredded clothing was strewn about her. Blood and signs of the struggle were everywhere. Firefinger could see from the marks around the farmer's wife that, with her last dregs of life she had tried to drag herself to her dying husband's side.

Firefinger silently communicated with those beings on the other side of life who could most help the farmer and his wife gently complete their transition into the Spirit Realm. A sense of warmth and well-being came over him as the Spirits of Medore and Emma were lovingly and gently surrounded, embraced, and lifted to their next level of being by the Nurturing Guardians of the Spirit Realm.

In the next moment, the very stars seemed to leave the sky and fill his head in a gently twinkling, swirling mist as he disconnected from the material world and moved his consciousness into the world of Spirit. From out of the depths of a blue mist appeared a vibrant, baby-blue glow. It began softly at first but strengthened and grew.

Barely discernible as it began, it became steadily more intense until it filled his perception, pushing everything else from his mind. With his inner vision, Firefinger became aware of the presence of the being that he had grown to know well and had come to call Blue Davol.

Blue Davol began moving toward him through the mists in his mind.

Davol, a tall wizened man of indeterminate but ancient years, wore a powder blue robe, a short, pointed blue hat and had a long white beard to match his long white hair. He had a very slight limp on his left side.

The apparition that was Davol approached through the mist in Firefinger's brain toward the perceiving eye in his mind that beheld this scene. From the first moment he had perceived Blue Davol, many years ago, Firefinger felt that he had always known this being. Although his hair and beard indicated great age, his face and his smooth movements indicated virile youth. This highly evolved and powerful being now spoke directly to Firefinger's mind.

Blue Davol wordlessly directed him to the back of the cottage where the farmers had lived. Behind a screen and next to the warmth of the small fireplace, under carefully folded and tucked bits of a shabby blanket, Firefinger was astonished to find a young boy, perhaps two years old, peacefully sleeping despite the carnage that had just destroyed his world.

Electrified; tingling from head to toe, Firefinger picked up the tiny boy in his blankets.

It was that deep soul-level tingling that occurred every time Spirit touched him with new knowledge and truth. In a kind and resonant voice, Firefinger was told this by the vision that was Davol, "Be alert so that no harm comes to this boy. Protect him, that nothing foul occurs to this babe, for he is more than you can know. His life means life for many, and with his word, he shall move mountains–and kingdoms. Anything that harms him harms the world to come, and yet, you are also charged with teaching him all that you know of living in and from the land, all of your woodcraft and hunting and fighting skills shall you teach this lad. Take this child and raise him as your own. Guard him, guide him, and protect him from all that would do him harm. Raise him in the ways of your elders, teach him the power and the craft of the world, the woods, the herbs, the flowers, the birds, the animals. Let him know all that there is to know and let him learn to respect all that lives, and all that supports those who live. This is your true purpose. This is why you walk the earth today. This is why you have chosen this incarnation. You are here to guard, guide, protect, nourish and educate this child. He is to be as your own son."

"...and one more thing, Firefinger." A mystical circular symbol blossomed from a blueish glow in Firefinger's mind.

Blazing brightly in his inner vision, the symbol of the heart within the circle branded itself forever into his memory. "When the time is right, I will return for this young man. You will know when it is appropriate to tell him of your history, and his, by this symbol. I will first come to him in his dreams. I will show him this identifying symbol so that it will validate all that you have told him and all that you have shown him about me. I will take him with me on soul journeys. I will show him the past, and I will show him the future. I will show him the wonders of the universe that exist within each and all of us. I will take him on travels through time and space, across dimensions, and between realities. I will show him that the only limitations that exist are those that we accept, and that, when we allow no restrictions, we become limitless.

In his blankets, you will find a clay disk with this emblem. It is his legacy. Keep it with him always.

I will make of him that which he has always been, and he shall be magnificent."

***

One day, twelve years later, while fishing with Firefinger, Chedrick found in the waters at his feet a flat rock with a curious symbol on it. The symbol was a circle containing a heart, both glowing with a soft, blue light. When Chedrick excitedly showed his find to Firefinger, the woodsman knew the time had come to speak to his son of the disc and the message that Blue Davol had given.

Telling his son the full story of his birth, Firefinger explained to Chedrick that he would be receiving some form of contact and communication that would take his skills and knowledge far beyond that which the woodsman could give him.

Beginning that night, Chedrick had the strangest dreams. He awoke in the morning knowing only that he had dreamed.

He did remember being told that, that which he was being taught would be available to him whenever he required it.

The teachings all lay buried in his mind against the day that they would be needed. As more time passed, he displayed surprising and intuitive skills in advanced herbalism, apparent miracles and healing gifts, and many other forms of esoteric knowledge. In addition, he began consciously exercising and learning more about his excellent and abundant natural gifts, and abilities of mind and Spirit.

Between his father's teachings and his own natural and impressive abilities, Chedrick's education in the ways of mind and Spirit was well underway by his 14th birthday. Even many years before the first hair would appear on his chin, his gifts were already every bit as impressive as his fabled father's.

CHAPTER 4—Firefinger is Born

Firefinger squatted in the gloom and watched the sleeping form of the boy, whom he had named Chedrick, breathing under the skins. He ruminated on the long and convoluted path that had brought him to this point in his own life.

It was in the early fall, nearly two years after the Dark Ones had exiled the old king and usurped the throne of Derf. What once had been a happy and prosperous kingdom suffered and dwindled under their selfish new ruler, King Luther the Dark.

King Luther and the Dark Lords quickly moved to drain the kingdom's treasuries into their own pockets and to bleed the farmers and merchants with outrageous new taxes, under the penalty of torture, death and forfeiture. The Dark Ones were agents of an evil cult born of politics and power, bent on destroying all beings and erasing all advanced knowledge that could challenge their earthly power and their vast fortunes. Greed was their God and blood and gold was His accepted sacrifice. There was no length they would not go to; there was no deed so foul that they would not utilize it to achieve and increase their power in the world. No citadel, village, farm, or castle was safe. Not even the most helpless child who might somehow or someday block their path was to be spared from the sword and the flames.

The Dark Ones traveled through the land and sowed seeds of suspicion, which became fear, which begat envy, distrust, jealousy, and finally hatred of all things "different."

Once hatred was born and nurtured, the Dark Ones had control and could easily lead the people to commit atrocities against their neighbors in the name of "defense."

That was a different world. Firefinger had, had another name then. He was called Adalbern, meaning "noble bear." His father naturally possessed phenomenal abilities of the mind, which Adalbern's upcoming advanced mystical energy training and education only enhanced.

Adalbern was a towheaded, curious, and smart lad. As he grew to manhood, his hair darkened, as so many do. He was a virtual sponge for knowledge and learning of every type. His early years were spent observing, gathering, retaining, and sorting all that the world and his parents could teach him.

Adalbern 's formal education in his people's ways began when he reached three years of age. For the first 16 years of his life, Adalbern helped his father around the farm and with the animals. They would go on extended hunting and fishing trips together to acquire provisions for the family. Adalbern did indeed become the skilled woodsman and hunter of which his father had dreamed.

Shortly before his 17th birthday, Adalbern set out into the world. He earned his new name when he was only 18 years of age, long before Chedrick was born. His new name was given to him by the inhabitants of the coastal town of Grimmor.

The town had the mixed fortune of being near important sea and land trade routes. The town of Grimmor had begun almost a century earlier as a small village on the western seacoast. It was the starting point of a trade route to the interior. Over the years it had become a major trade center with all of the good and all of the bad that, that brings. Great wealth, lawlessness, high poverty, and great greed all stalked the streets. Its location invited not only caravans laden with the riches of the world, but merchant vessels, rich with cargo for the caravans to take away and distribute. The ships stayed busy reloading with the caravans' treasures to take them to other parts of the world after unloading their precious cargos into Grimmor. It was a town with a plethora of pirates, grifters, gamblers, and thieves who preyed on those merchants, the traders, and the townspeople, as a way of life.

The Lords of Grimmor had been put on notice by the Sea Merchants Guild that their ships would no longer stop in the port so long as the rampaging pirates were not stopped.

Because of his ever-growing reputation as a Mage, and despite his youth, Adalbern was summoned by the village's leadership to put an end to the death and destruction on the high seas once and for all. The timing was important, because one last flotilla, a veritable armada of merchant ships traveling together for their joint safety, would soon be entering the port of Grimmor.

Forewarned by a mercenary on one of the armada's vessels, a flotilla of pirates nearly equal in size to the merchant fleet approached the bay. Working together in a rare show of strength and unity, the pirate fleet sailed into the bay only hours after the armada had dropped anchor, and blocked the harbor. Then began the hell of the Grimmor Bay Massacre. The pirates sailed into the bay, attacking the armada with fire and fury.

This grand fleet of merchant ships was to be a prize beyond all prizes, a treasure beyond all treasures, should they win the day.

For two full days, the battle raged. Fire arrows were rained down on both sides like hellish hail. Catapults flung tightly-wrapped oil-soaked bundles of burning rags. Explosive charges wrapped in oilcloth with a double handful of small sharp stones at the center of the rags, next to an explosive charge that would strip flesh from bones when they exploded on enemy decks.

Casualties were heavy on both sides. Many ships were burning, sunk, or badly damaged.

Far into the night, the battle raged, until darkness and smoke obliterated the enemies from each other's sight.

As dawn whispered its first tendrils of light on the third morning, the air once again was filled with missiles flying in both directions and the screams of the injured and dying.

Late in the evening of the second day of the battle, when night had fallen and it was once again too dark to fight, Adalbern appeared at the edge of the village, dressed in his dirty forest-green cloak, the shabby cowl pulled over his weathered head to hide his distinctive and craggy, handsome features.

Moving silently, he made his way to the meeting place

set up by the Lords of Grimmor on the outskirts of town, away from the center. Arriving at the house that had been described in the message he had received from the trusted messenger that morning before daybreak, he knocked on the door and was admitted into the darkened room.

All around him there was a sudden rustling and a shuffling as men sleeping the sleep of exhaustion roused themselves to speak with him.

Although the Lords of Grimmor had seen many things in their lives and had heard many stories of Adalbern's abilities, none were prepared to believe his claims of what he could accomplish. After much heated discussion, accompanied finally by small demonstrations of his remarkable skills, just before daybreak, Adalbern finally convinced them to trust him. The Lords of Grimmor accepted his seemingly impossible plan to defeat the pirate fleet.

They really had no options.

In the predawn hours, Adalbern stepped back out into the street and began walking purposefully toward the small hill on the outside of town that overlooked the bay. The Lords of Grimmor slunk out moments later, following gingerly, and with fear and hesitation, in the shadow of Adalbern 's passage.

Alone that morning, he made his way to the top of the small hill overlooking the bay. The Lords of Grimmor slunk behind him in the semi-darkness and cowered beneath the trees at a safe distance in order to witness what was to come.

As the sun began its journey over the mountain tops, illuminating the scene before him, Adalbern was just able to make out the pirate fleet with his eyes.

Summoning all of his knowledge and harnessing all of his powers, he pointed his finger at the pirate ships, focused his mind, and gathered his energies. Rapidly a glowing mist formed a brilliant red-gold sphere of energy at the tip of his finger. The sphere then sped unerringly toward the hapless ship he was pointing to.

Ship after pirate ship burst into flame as the fiery energy pulse struck it. Each ship rapidly burned to the waves, then quickly sank to the bottom of the sea, as though it had been constructed of lead. The pirate fleet was utterly destroyed, burnt and crushed, demolished, in a matter of minutes.

Those aboard the stricken pirate vessels perished in the resulting conflagrations.

There was mass chaos and screams from the crews on ships not yet destroyed, as they watched the swift and soundless destruction of their mates.

CHAPTER 5—On Board the Golden Goose

Bung, the wiry, pasty-faced 14-year-old powder monkey, struggled up from below decks on the Golden Goose, a three-masted Carrack ship of the pirate fleet. In his right hand was a leather bucket with the last load of shot for the ship's demi-culverin cannon near the mizzenmast. Moving slowly, as he had been up all night and working hard, he carried the heavy bucket aft and stacked the shot into a pyramid of iron. The last load of cannonballs finally arranged, Bung dared to take a momentary break, after working all night preparing for the day's battle.

Bung had been born a nobody. He had been abandoned by his derelict mother at a very young age and raised in the gutters by the other orphans of the streets. In this hard school of survival, he had learned to beg and steal, and had once even murdered a man who caught him in the act of lifting his purse! Despite his survival training, Bung was not quite smart enough or fast enough to escape the small band of goons who were looking for 'volunteers' to do the lowly tasks that keep a pirate ship running. He had been drugged with a doctored piece of stale bread and kidnapped. Before he awakened from the drug's effects, he had been taken onto this very ship in a port very far away from here. Life on board was hard, but so was he, and this life was better than any he had ever known. He was proud to be a pirate!

Standing in the near-total darkness and leaning over the rail for a moment he gazed through the dark distance at the barely discernable profile of hills outlined by the imminent rising of the sun. Bung was exhausted by the long night's labors.

His blank, unthinking stare suddenly found a focus.

His attention was captured and his curiosity engaged by the appearance of a tiny orange spark of light near the top of the nearest hill, a small bright light that seemed to grow swiftly against the semi-darkness behind it.

As he watched, it continued to grow very rapidly until it filled his entire world with bright orange light.

"It's going to hit us!" he thought to himself.

Bung's childhood friend, Cole, was roping the last of the powder kegs together on the Cutlass, anchored just a hundred yards to port from the Golden Goose. He had just enough time to begin to notice the bright glow in the air about him before the ball of fire, speeding through the night sky, hit his ship, instantly engulfing it and everyone on board. There was not a sound as the ship and its crew were engulfed and quickly dissolved in a ball of raging orange fire.

Bung gawked in disbelief as the blinding fireball sped past his ship and struck the Cutlass. "It looks like a thousand angry sea serpents slithering over one another," his stunned mind thought. There was no sound; no screams heard from the Cutlass as the fireball flared, then dissipated to nothingness, leaving only ash on the water, and a small whirlpool where the ship had been a moment before.

When Bung's vision returned, there was nothing left of the Cutlass above the waterline. Everything above the waterline was gone in an instant. Then, as though grasped by the hand of an invisible demon from beneath, the husk of the Cutlass had been dragged beneath the waves. Only a few small tongues of flame were visible in the rapidly sinking wreckage.

So transfixed was he on the fate of the Cutlass, he never saw the ball of fire that struck his own ship, the Golden Goose.

The Lords of Grimmor, who were lurking in the shadows behind Adalbern, watched in awe and disbelief. This event was far beyond their expectation. The entire scene was far beyond anything they had ever experienced. Had they not seen it with their own eyes, smelled the burning ships, and heard the screaming of the pirate sailors, they never would have believed it. Excitedly, they spoke among themselves about the wonder of the writhing spheres of fire that leaped from Adalbern's finger and how it had destroyed their enemies so quickly and completely.

At that moment, Adalbern ceased to be and Firefinger was born.

CHAPTER 6—The Hunt

Firefinger's name and fame grew like wildfire throughout the land. His name was spoken in reverent whispers in back alleys. Minstrels sang to his glory in ale houses and castles alike. Stories of his many achievements abounded and surpassed even his substantial abilities to make them real.

Such a remarkable man could not long maintain anonymity. It was only a matter of time before the Dark Ones learned of Firefinger.

Hearing the many tales of Firefinger's achievements, it was quickly determined by the Dark Ones that he represented a sizable threat to their power and their greedy goals. It was quickly decided by the greedy and evil forces behind the Dark Ones that their version of the world would be far better if Firefinger did not live in it.

Firefinger should be killed.

From the castle of the Dark Ones came an edict, and the offer of a great reward. Land, livestock, and gold for the head of Firefinger!

For five more years, Firefinger was only a legend in most of the world. He was a ghost that could not be seen. Because of his awareness and gifts, he was always a step away from his enemies and could not be touched by the Dark Ones. He traveled with impunity through the world, moving quietly and quickly. In the course of each day his legend grew. Healing a lame horse, a lame cow, or a farmer cursed with the dreaded wasting sickness was an everyday event. Wherever he went in this world, life for the villagers improved.

Teaching others to do some of the things he did, and sharing his knowledge with the people of the villages was one of the many reasons that he was so loved. A Mage, a healer, a teacher, and ever an observer and a student, he moved through his world.

His private thoughts often took him to memories of his father, mother, and their modest home and lands in his far-away homeland of Racerio in a quiet valley between mountain ranges. In those moments he missed his parents, their land, the family's farm, the mountains, and the animals of his childhood, but there was much to be done in the world, and his drive to help others outweighed his loneliness.

Born of the southern people, his family was massacred in a treacherous raid by the Dark Ones when he was but 17, and already on his own in the world. His youth suddenly disappeared, making him a man before his time.

Late one night, shortly after falling asleep, Firefinger was suddenly jolted awake by an awareness that his mother was in great fear and pain. Firefinger felt within his own body the fiery thrust of a dagger into her breast. As he tried to catch his breath, he felt a sword rampage through her bedclothes into her belly, severing her spine as it exited the other side. The mortal wound leaves her gasping out her last breath, lying in a growing pool of blood. As he reached out with his mind to touch that of his father's, he felt the last flicker of light in that magnificent mind go dark in death as well. Fully awake now, he could see with his inner vision the cadre of the Dark Ones' minions roiling over the hills and through their once-tranquil pasture into and through the place he had once called home. Unsuccessful in their attempts to kill Firefinger, the league of the Dark Ones had sacrificed his parents and had looted and burned all in their spite.

The Dark Ones then began a deliberate campaign to turn the people against their hero. They spread lie after lie and sowed seeds of suspicion against Firefinger in all the villages throughout the land. He was called a witch, a warlock, an evil Spirit incarnate. Many false tales were told. He was even said to eat live infants.

The Dark Ones carefully tended and nurtured those tainted and shadowed seeds of falsehoods until they grew into fear in the minds of the weakest members of the populace.

Once that fear had been kindled, it brought with it distrust, and finally from that fear was born hatred. Once that unthinking hatred had fully blossomed and had spread its stink throughout the land, the Dark Ones could easily lead the people to commit almost any atrocities against themselves and one another in the name of protection from the hideous specter that now, in their undiscerning minds, was Firefinger.

Having brought the public's fear and hatred of Firefinger to the boiling point, the next step in their plan was implemented, and notices were posted on every tree in every village offering a rich reward for the head of the foul evildoer, Firefinger.

Late in the fall, when the days are short and the nights long, after a long day and evening of carousing and ale, a ragtag band of the roughest villagers from Burbarrow decided that they would capture Firefinger's head and split the massive treasure. Firefinger had been known to be in the area for the past several days, healing, teaching, and helping the locals in whatever way he could. He supped each night in one of three taverns in the area. The drunken, plotting villagers set out to put an end to the evil that was Firefinger once and for all, and to make themselves rich in the process.

There was a man named Groswald, from Burbarrow, whose wife had been saved from a terrible death during a very difficult childbirth three years earlier by Firefinger's herbs and energy healing skills. Secretly a supporter of Firefinger, he joined the group of plotters and listened intently as they made plans for their clumsy trap.

CHAPTER 7—A Dastardly Deed, Indeed

One of the leaders of that rowdy group carried the name of Clodwig. He was a great hairy giant of a man. Dark, brooding, and threatening at the best of times, Clodwig lived with a woman who was a server at the Broken Flagon, where Firefinger was seen to eat most often when he visited the town.

When next Firefinger was there, she was to slip a sleep-inducing potion into his horn of mead and send word to the others waiting nearby when that deed had been accomplished. The band of miscreants would then move closer to the Broken Flagon and hide outside until she gave the second signal telling them that Firefinger had lost consciousness and their success was assured. When Firefinger was harmless, they would storm into the Broken Flagon and bind him securely before spiriting him away to a small meadow where the fire had already been laid. There could be no chances taken when dealing with a prisoner with such legendary skills and gifts. They would take him then into the woods outside of town and finish him. They would take his head and make themselves legendary and wealthy!

They would be RICH!

Little did they know that there was a large portion of the public who knew and revered Firefinger; he who had healed their mother, worked beside them to repair a fence, or taught them the ways of herbal medicine.

Those who knew Firefinger knew that all of the Dark Ones' lies were just that. Most would do almost anything to protect him. One such person, Halt Eagom, heard the rowdy boasting and loud threats from the villagers of Burbarrow. Scurrying away from the house, he borrowed a horse from Groswald, another of Firefinger's secret supporters. Halt Eagom then rode off into the forest to warn Firefinger of the villager's plans.

CHAPTER 8—The Deed Is Done

Two days later, after a day of teaching followed by an evening assisting a farmer whose mare had fallen ill, Firefinger made his way to the Broken Flagon for a well-deserved hot meal and a horn of mead.

Aldith, Clodwig's equally repugnant woman, saw Firefinger come through the door of the tavern on her way back to the kitchen. Walking out the back door, she made a great show of banging a metal spoon on the bottom of a pot, notifying the gang's lackey of Firefinger's arrival.

As the runner scurried off to take his message to Clodwig, Aldith prepared the potion for Firefinger's mead. Scuttling out to his table, she placed the horn of toxic mead in front of him. Chatting pleasantly with him as he drank the potion, she kept her eye peeled for the first signs that it was taking effect. Fairly quickly, Firefinger's eyes glazed over, and his head nodded, then fell heavily towards the table, landing squarely on the shepherd's pie that she had brought with the mead.

Waiting a few more moments for any sign of movement and seeing none, she boldly reached out and pinched his cheek hard. There was no sign of consciousness. Emboldened, she struck the side of his head with her dirty cleaning cloth wrapped around her grimy fist. Still, there was no response.

Stepping into the street, she waved that same rag over her head and called the motley band of would-be murderers into the Broken Flagon.

Stepping quickly up to the doorway, where they seem to lose their courage, Clodwig and his band entered the tavern with trepidation and caution. Seeing Firefinger slumped over his table with his face in his shepherd's pie was too much for Clodwig. Viewing the apparent success of his plan after days of anticipation and stress caused him to break into hysterical laughter for a few moments. His band of ruffians stepped back and looked at their leader with great confusion. Recovering quickly, Clodwig began barking orders at his men.

In a trice, Firefinger was blindfolded and bound. His unresponsive body was dragged unceremoniously into the street where two ruffians tied him crosswise onto the back of a horse. Curious onlookers witnessed the scene but dared not interfere, knowing Clodwig's reputation for fiery anger and sudden violence.

Into the forest the group rode, finally arriving at the hidden meadow. Scarcely believing their luck, they cut down Firefinger's body from the saddle. Still bound, still unconscious, this fabled mage and warrior presented no apparent threat to them. Stepping forward while two of their party held Firefinger upright, Clodwig wrapped his fingers in Firefinger's brown locks, held his head high, and swiftly drew the sharp knife from ear to ear in one swift and deep stroke. Stepping back, he nodded to his lieutenants and they let Firefinger's body fall to the earth.

Satisfied with their success, at last, Clodwig resigned his two lieutenants to finish the job and remove Firefinger's head. Once his throat was slit, his head removed and his body thrown into a pyre of wood, coals, and flames, the revelry began in earnest.

The bloody grinning head was jammed onto a sharpened wooden pole and set into a hole in the ground next to the fire. The celebration and raucous shouting of the rowdy band could be heard well into the night and into the morning hours.

Firefinger watched all this from the shadows at the edge of the forest next to the stump. Finally, he was free!

Nearly an hour later as he was moving through the woods, he heard an owl, the prearranged signal from his friends and supporters from the town.

Clodwig had taken his prize, the head of Firefinger, placed it in a burlap bag tied to his saddle, and had ridden off toward the capital city where the Dark Lords and his reward awaited him.

As soon as Clodwig was safely out of earshot, Firefinger

sent a mental command to the revelers celebrating his death.

"Those who were once your friends are now your enemies," he said in their minds. "Think how much more reward you would have if they were all dead!"

The drunken oafs, who had been lifelong friends in many cases, suddenly looked about themselves and saw naught but enemies. In their blind greed they used knives, stones, fists, and large burning branches; whatever came to hand. A grand melee ensued until, at last, every last man lay dead or mortally injured.

Firefinger's friends, hiding in the woods and observing as the last of the foul murderers fell to the earth in death, once again gave the prearranged owl hoot, a signal to Firefinger that his revenge had been exacted on the perpetrators by themselves.

CHAPTER 9—Clodwig's Reward

Moving through the thin edge of the forest toward the road that led to the capital, Clodwig could feel behind him on his right flank, the steady thump, thump, thump of Firefinger's head as it kept time with the horses' hooves.

"Those fools," thought Clodwig. "Those crazy, drunken fools. I'm off to the capital with Firefinger's head. I alone shall collect the prize. I shall be wealthy beyond belief and they will never see me again. Not one of them was smart enough or sober enough to think to come with me to protect their part of the prize." Clodwig roared with laughter at having pulled off such a marvelous coup. His future was assured, and he would be wealthy beyond his wildest dreams!

After two long days of travel by horseback, Clodwig arrived in the capital. Riding up to the city's gate, he demanded of the guards to be taken before the Dark Ones.

"Who do you think you are," asked the tallest and burliest of the gate guards.

"I have important business with the Dark Ones, and I must see them soon!" Clodwig demanded. The head in his bag was beginning to smell quite badly and constantly leaked noxious fluids through the course fabric to drip on the ground. "I bring them the head of Firefinger," he proclaimed, holding the soiled, bulging bag up for them to view.

"One moment," the biggest guard said. "Let me see what's in the bag."

Reluctantly, Clodwig untied the top of the heavily soiled and leaking bag and opened it under the guard's nose. The guard looked in the bag quickly, retched and turned on his heel, and disappeared into the guard station. A moment later he returned with the captain of the guard. The captain was half a head taller than most men, heavily muscled, heavily scarred, and stinking of several days' of sweat that had stained his tunic.

"Show me," he demanded. Again, Clodwig held open the bag so that the captain of the guard could see for himself the head of Firefinger.

"Follow me," said the captain as he turned and walked back into the guard station. "Wait here."

Clodwig sat alone in the guard station as the captain disappeared into the labyrinth of stone tunnels and passages which led to the Dark Ones' castle.

In the close quarters of the room, the stench from the bag became almost overpowering. After what seemed like forever, the captain returned, glanced at Clodwig, and ordered, "Follow me!"

Scrambling to his feet after sitting for so long, Clodwig almost stumbled. "Hurry up!" bellowed a loud voice from somewhere in front of him in the semi-lit tunnels. "Hurry up!"

The passages were so narrow that Clodwig was forced to carry his onerous burden in his arms against his chest as he hustled to try to keep up with the captain. First left, then right, then right again, then left, he chased diminishing footsteps ahead of him in an effort to keep up with the captain.

Finally, turning a corner at full speed, he nearly bumped into the captain face-to-face as the captain stood waiting for him in front of a doorway.

"When you go through this door, there will be three guards. One will stand ready to kill you at a moment's notice. The other two will search you for weapons. If you survive the search, you will be brought before the Dark Ones. I suggest you be respectful and forthright." With that, the captain opened the door and escorted Clodwig through to experience the not-so-tender mercies of the guards.

After the quick, thorough, and none too gentle search, Clodwig with his odiferous but precious parcel was told to sit on a stone bench until another door opened that would bring him face-to-face with the Dark Lords.

As Clodwig sat and waited, the bag dripping on the stone floor as he sat there, he heard raised voices coming from the other side of the door. Although he could not make out the words, he thought the voices sounded excited and happy. "I'm going to be rich! I'm going to live like a king!"

The door opened. Two burly and heavily armed guards motioned for Clodwig to come into the room. Five steps into the room and 20 steps away from the three thrones on a raised platform, the guards motioned for him to stop.

"So, these are the great Dark Lords," Clodwig thought to himself. "Why, they don't look powerful at all. They look like ordinary men sitting on those thrones."

Suddenly a heavy boot was placed in the small of his back and he was shoved forward toward the thrones so rudely that he stumbled for three steps and fell sprawling. The bag hit the floor, and the disgusting, festering head rolled toward the throne. It might've been chance or it might've been fate, but when the bag and the head came to a stop, the head was staring straight at the Dark Lords. The eyes were open, and the lips were pulled back in a ghastly grin. The bag had settled around the head, framing it in soiled burlap. A most impressive picture, indeed.

Scrambling to his feet, Clodwig approached the Dark Lords, standing next to the head on the floor. "Sirs, kind sirs, noble sirs, I have brought you the head of Firefinger, and I have come to claim my reward."

The Dark Lord on the right side of the platform turned to his right and gave a signal to a waiting lackey, who then disappeared through the door behind them, and immediately returned with an old woman in tow.

"You! Old woman! Come here. Look at this face," the Lord commanded as he pointed to Firefinger's head on the floor. "Who is this? Do you know this man? Speak up, now!"

Cringing, the old woman shuffled toward the head on the floor. She looked at it and began weeping piteously. "This is Adalbern! You have killed Firefinger!"

As the old woman was unceremoniously dragged, wailing and weeping, back through the door she had entered moments before, the Dark Lord in the center of the stage motioned to

Clodwig to approach.

"You have done well, Claudeson," he said, purposefully using the wrong name. An evil grin crossed the Dark Lords' face. "I suppose now you want your reward?"

Beside himself with greed, Clodwig nodded vigorously. Silently, the Dark Lord motioned with a hand gesture to the guards.

Marching up to Clodwig's position, the guards stationed themselves; one on each side, and each firmly grasped an arm. Perhaps the steely grip that each guard imposed upon his biceps was the first inclination that things may not be going quite as swimmingly as Clodwig had thought they might have.

The two guards and their prisoner turned and walked toward the door through which Clodwig had initially entered. Once through the door, however, the guards' grips did not lighten. The trio turned right and awkwardly went down a previously unnoticed narrow corridor that led to the dungeon.

The guards began laughing at Clodwig's panicked reaction. "Don't worry, you won't be here long," the guard on his left told him with a nasty chuckle.

"At most, you'll only be here a couple of days," laughed the guard on his right. "Just long enough to build the gibbet."

It was not quite two days before Clodwig was removed from the dungeon. Frightened and hungry, he was led through the castle to a tower. A massive metal pole extended on the outside of the tower and a metal cage the size and shape of a man sat on the floor next to the window.

The two guards nudged one another with knowing grins. "Here's your reward, oh killer of Firefinger! You will have the best view of our city for the rest of your life!"

Grabbing Clodwig most roughly, they forced him into the metal cage and, using ropes and pulleys, moved him out onto the metal pole to hang at the end. Ignored, Clodwig would remain dangling there in that cage until long after his Spirit had gone from his flesh, the flesh had gone from his bones, and the bones were picked clean by the birds and the insects, until, one by one, they fell through the grate onto passersby below.

CHAPTER 10—Chedrick Awakens

It had taken every bit of Firefinger's knowledge, abilities, and strength to create another body for the purpose of fooling his enemies, but the results were well worth the effort.

Bilocation was something only the most experienced of adepts could attempt. Bilocation with soul separation, as he had done in this case, was something only the most advanced and experienced adept could hope to accomplish.

By successfully creating another instance of himself and choosing to allow it to be sacrificed to buy his freedom, Firefinger became a living legend. By calling back the small portion of his soul which had inhabited that other body, at the very last instant of its life, he remained intact.

Chedrick stirred under the sleeping robes that covered him as he slept on the leaves that he had gathered and piled on the soft forest floor. He was a strong lad, now having almost 14 years, most of it living as a woodsman. Already, Firefinger could see the handsome man his son was to become. Tall, smart, agile, and strong, with a shock of tawny almost-blonde hair and blue eyes that could pierce the night.

Gently, lovingly, Firefinger touched his son on the cheek. Chedrick's eyes opened, then opened even wider as he recognized from his father's energy that something of major importance had occurred.

Although Chedrick was very aware of some of his father's abilities, he was far from being fully trained. Thus, he was unaware of the full extent and phenomenal scope of Firefinger's gifts.

"Son," Firefinger said, "we're free now. We can stop running. The Dark Ones now believe that I am dead and they will not hunt us anymore."

"But father," Chedrick protested, "you told me last night

that they were getting too close. You told me that there was great danger. What happened?"

"Chedrick, there are many skills you have yet to learn. There are things that even you do not yet understand or even know of, that are part of my everyday world. There is so much of our family history that I have not yet shared with you. I have the knowledge of the ancients. I use the gifts my star blood offers. I used all that I am and all that I have to create another body. To make another ME.

I allowed that other body to be sacrificed to their blood-lust, to their greed.

That other body has bought our freedom."

"I don't understand, father. How were these things even possible? What is Star Blood? What is the knowledge of the ancients? When can I learn it? How can I learn it?"

Firefinger chuckled gently and allowed himself to fall back onto a pile of furs. Resting on one elbow, he continued his conversation with his son. "I think it is time for breakfast. We shall speak of these things later. In the meantime, study your books. Books will give you access to the thoughts of the great minds of all times."

Firefinger had acquired and given Chedrick five rustic volumes, handwritten on vellum, containing knowledge both common and esoteric. They were treasures beyond measure, passed from scholar to student for many generations.

That evening, Chedrick asks again. "Father, when can I find out more about the ancients? When can I learn what you know?"

"That is not to be determined by me. Spirit will come to you in its own way and in its own time. The Ancient Ones live on in the Spirit realm and visit those who are worthy. When the time is right, you will meet them, son. Of that you can be sure," Firefinger said gently as he tucked Chedrick in for the night. "I feel your time is near. When the student is ready, the teacher appears, and when the student is truly ready, the teacher disappears. Just remember this: 'It is not always wise for those who control great power to display it openly.' There are those who will be your friends in their ignorance, but will fear and avoid you, in their knowledge."

CHAPTER 11—Dream Worlds

Sometime later, midway in his 14th year, and many miles away, Chedrick awakens one morning from a strange dream.

"Father, I had the most unusual dream last night. I seemed to be floating in nothingness, when suddenly, in front of me there was a glow, a bright blue glow that came to fill my entire dream world. In the dream, I heard a voice that told me: 'Awaken, Chedrick. Awaken. It is time.' What can it mean, father?"

"Chedrick," his father said, "was there anything more about the dream that you remember?"

"I remember very little of the dream. I remember the voice, the glow, and a feeling that all was well in that world."

Firefinger sat down on a small pile of furs and motioned for Chedrick to sit beside him. "It is time now, son, to tell you of your birth, your heritage, and your destiny." Gently, Firefinger told his son for the first time the story of how he had found the toddler next to the fireplace in his parents' home. Firefinger spoke of the vision, of Blue Davol and his message.

"After that," Firefinger said, "I made it a point to find out about your birthright and your lineage. I knew the day would come when it was time to let you know who you really are. I want you to know that you are the son of my heart but not my loins. It makes no difference. I could not love you more than I do each day. You are my life and my reason for being. Here is what I know of your story, of your heritage."

"Chedrick, your great-grandfather six times removed was Jagen of Derf." Firefinger began reciting in almost a sing-song voice the tale he had pieced together from the information given by the crofters and townspeople near the ill-fated farm in Derf where he found the boy. It was the litany of Chedrick's earthly pedigree.

"Jagen was born of Mathelde the Small, daughter of the Grand Mage of Derf and of Ariel, one of the last surviving members of the Lemurian Ancient Ones.

Gelephon, Arial's father, was of the Star People. He sat on the great council of Lemuria for 1200 years.

Arial was, like all of his race, a master of mind and Spirit. His Star blood and off-world education set him far above his peers, even in those days. He was tall among men, with blue eyes and blonde hair with strong but pleasant features. Most common folk today would call him a Mage or a Wizard, but what is rare today was common then. His people, ancient beyond reckoning, had long known and practiced these gifts and talents. Each generation had passed their knowledge to the next, as I have begun to do with you. When the Ancient Ones come to you, you will learn far more than what my humble teachings can offer.

Jagen was one of the last of a forgotten race from a forgotten land, now hidden deep beneath the ocean's waves. That land was called Lemuria, and Jagen's people were rumors and legends even in that antique land. The Lemurians called them the Ancient Ones because of their very, very long lives and the fact that they had walked the earth in small numbers since before Man's memories began. Eons earlier they had mastered mind and Spirit and lived in peace and harmony with themselves, with one another. They were at peace with the forest, the planet, and all who dwelt there. Performing remarkable and impossible things was part of their everyday life. No one wanted for anything, and Love was the ruler of their land."

"Jagen and Mathelde's only child, Dinor, was raised in the castle of Derf and brought up skilled and knowledgeable in the ancient ways of his father. When he reached young adulthood, he traveled and explored the world.

During his journeys, and unknown to him, Derf was overrun, and all the occupants of the royal compound were slaughtered like sheep, including his parents. The castle was razed to the ground and the stones scattered across the landscape. Alone now in the world, Dinor moved on, married, and had a child, Fenner, to whom he passed the ancient knowledge passed down from generations before.

And so it went, until you, Chedrick.

I have raised you in the old ways, and I have given you all the knowledge that is mine to give. Time will give you the experiences and confidence to make the most of what I have given and what you have yet to learn."

"But father! Where is Derf, what is Lemuria, and who are the Ancient Ones? Can I meet one?"

Chedrick's eyes glinted in the campfire's light. "When can I meet an Ancient One, father?" he repeated.

CHAPTER 12—The Dream World Beckons

It was a beautiful night in the forest. The air was warm and the night was quiet except for the subtle scurrying of the night creatures going about their business of hunting and harvesting, hiding, and mating.

Chedrick walked the moonlit path that wandered among the trees. A large toad, sitting on a huge mushroom, waved hello to him and bid him a good evening. "And a good evening to you as well, Mr. Toad."

"Fran," the toad replied. "Fran Gel."

"Excuse me?" Chedrick asked.

"Fran Gel. It's my name. Fran Gel, and I'm a Miss."

Chedrick nodded to the toad as he passed. "Have a wonderful night, Fran Gel," and continued on his journey.

The cloudless sky shimmered with stars and the full moon looked down on the forest, casting its silvery light on the tranquil scene.

A short way into the distance, a small blue spark flitted furtively from tree to tree. Chedrick never quite saw it directly. Instead, it teased his eyes, always just out of sight, tickling his peripheral vision. In each instance, his alert nature caused his head to turn in that direction, knowing that there was something there, but never quite being able to catch it with his vision.

Suddenly, it came rushing down the path toward him, filling his vision, nay, flooding his world with a blinding, bright-blue light the size of a melon floating three feet in front of his face.

As bright as the light was, at its heart was an orb of even brighter blue, glistening with a vibrant beauty. It was as much brighter from the blinding blue light that surrounded it as that light was from the moonlight that had dominated the scene a moment before.

As quickly as it had come, the light faded into nothingness, and Chedrick stirred and turned over in his sleep. There were other dreams that night; ordinary dreams, busy dreams that meant nothing and cluttered his mind. By morning the amazing experience was but a faint but persistent memory.

Life went on. Chedrick had all but forgotten the powerful dream of the week before. His life was full with the gathering of herbs for medications and potions; honing his woodcraft and survival skills for life in the deep forest. Firefinger kept him very busy learning all that he had to teach.

After a particularly exhausting day, Chedrick collapsed onto his bed and fell almost instantly into a deep sleep. He had not been asleep long when the dream of the week before replayed itself before his inner eyes.

There were differences this time. Subtle differences to begin with. Again, the toad greeted him as he passed. He had not noticed before the faint blue glow that outlined Miss Toad.

"You have returned," Miss Toad observed. "Did you enjoy your last visit? There is far more to see on this path than you could ever imagine.

Enjoy your stroll, for it leads to the door of your future." The toad laughed a resonant and mellifluous laugh as she winked out of existence with a little blue 'poof.'

Taking this strange occurrence in stride, knowing in his dream that it was a dream, Chedrick continued down the path toward the spot where the light had first appeared in his previous dream. Even further down the path, around a corner and over a small rise, he came upon a remarkable scene.

As he topped the crest of the small rise on his path, he saw before him what appeared to be a translucent blue veil, shimmering lightly and stretching across his entire field of vision. It was almost as though it were a doorway to another world, another reality.

As he walked forward, toward the veil, it retreated a step for every step he took, refusing him entrance to the world beyond, taunting him with its nearness and its novelty.

And a magical world it appeared to be. Sophisticated

buildings made of stone, simple yet elegant, like the ancient temples Firefinger had told him about. Wherever he looked, people were casually walking beautiful paths of smooth cobblestones towards destinations unknown. Those who were dressed wore short, translucent clothing of odd design. Most were barefoot, although some wore simple sandals. The people were robust but not fat or overly muscular. They were a handsome people, overall. They did not notice him. Perhaps they could not see him. There was an instant, just a moment, when it seemed that a tall old man with a long white beard, dressed in a sky-blue robe and a short blue hat seemed to notice him as he walked close by, along the path to whatever destination he was seeking. But, no.

There was no spark of recognition and the old man continued his meandering walk, a sly smile touching the corners of his mouth for a moment. Chedrick continued his vigil and watched in fascination for what seemed like a long time before this vision also faded from his sight, and he awakened from his sleep.

Fully awake now, Chedrick rose from his sleeping pelts, stretched luxuriously, and, because it was still hours before daylight, stepped forward onto a favorite path through the woods toward their creek.

He had always enjoyed solitary walks in the moonlight through the living forest. Other than his footsteps, the only sounds were the occasional hoot of an owl or swift scurrying of its intended prey. But when he stopped, stood still, and listened with his inner ear, he could hear the trees speaking to one another, the worms emerging briefly from the rich, brown earth. He could hear the insects conversing in their near-silent language. It was at times such as these, that Chedrick felt most connected to the woods, this world, and the world beyond.

After standing for some moments in his silent reverie, Chedrick resumed his ramble among the ancient moss-covered oaks of the forest, along his favorite path that led to a tiny, verdant meadow that only he and Firefinger knew of. It was their very own secret, sacred, sanctum sanctorum, where they did their deepest and clearest thinking.

It was calling him tonight.

CHAPTER 13—Everything Changes

This night was clear, cloudless. The full moon shone softly, creating a pleasant, unearthly illumination. The deep-blue sky above him, marking the hours just before dawn, was filled with the brightest, clearest stars he could remember.

Stepping over a moss-covered log, careful to avoid a sleeping toad, Chedrick crossed the small meadow to a favorite rock, one which seemed to have been shaped to exactly fit his bottom. Covered with a dense growth of moss, it had proved over the years to be exceedingly comfortable for long sits. He could hear their stream in the near distance.

Chedrick sat there, mindlessly staring off into space, listening to the inner dialogue of the forest. His mind was relaxed and open, attentive, but not intense, like a sponge waiting languidly for whatever nurturing the universe and that night might bring him.

He did not have to wait for long.

A slight, bright movement at the periphery of his vision imposed itself on his reverie. He quickly looked down towards his left foot, where he thought he had seen something, but nothing was there.

Returning to his reverie, he found himself reviewing tales that he had been told by Firefinger and others about the realms of energy, and the innate powers of all men to harness energy for the benefit of all.

There was again!

Looking down quickly, Chedrick saw the quick disappearance of a tiny bright blue spark, near the big toe of his left foot. This time, he kept watching.

As if on cue, a brightly glowing, vibrant-blue worm crawled out of the soil and onto his foot.

"It's odd, I know, but I could swear that worm is looking

at me," he thought, incredulously.

No sooner had he thought that, then the worm grew to trice its previous size, sprouting limbs, a head, and a face.

...And that face WAS looking at him!

It kept growing! In a moment's time, the glowing blue worm had become a tiny Dragon, complete with wings, tail, and limbs.

. . .And it was scrambling rapidly up his left shin toward his knee.

Chedrick discovered that he was remaining remarkably calm, considering the extraordinary event happening on his leg. He sat and patiently waited until the Dragon arranged itself on his knee. It ruffled its wings slightly, circled like a cat about to nap, and settled itself into a comfortable position facing Chedrick.

"Good morning, my boy! I have been waiting to meet you for so long. I am here to open your doors, to change your life beyond measure, and to help you to transform yourself into what you have always been," the now not-so-tiny blue Dragon said, as it continued to grow larger.

The Dragon's voice carried far more weight than volume. When Truth is spoken, it does not need to shout. Chedrick recognized in an instant that this Dragon spoke Truth.

"Sir Dragon," Chedrick replied, "it is beyond my wildest dreams to meet you, even though, before this instant, I knew not of your existence. What may I call you, sir?"

The Dragon doubled in size once more, now becoming the size of a very large house cat. It chortled.

If you have never heard a vibrant blue Dragon chortle, then your life is truly impoverished.

It had the warmth of a best friend, the love of a grandmother, the wisdom of the sage, and the power of the universe. It felt like encouragement and best wishes, wrapped in warmth and surety.

The Dragon appeared to grin, broadly, then burped loudly. The burp was visible–bright vibrant blue light. It floated above the d\Dragon's head and swiftly took the form of a heart within a circle–the symbol Chedrick had heard many stories about from Firefinger.

"Allow me to introduce myself," the Dragon said.

There was a silent, spectacular explosion of vibrant blue light, and when Chedrick regained his faculties, there stood before him a stately man dressed in robes. He glowed; he radiated the vibrant baby-blue light that Chedrick was becoming so familiar with. He was nearly a head taller than Chedrick, well-built, despite his obvious age. His flowing white hair cascaded slightly beyond his shoulders, and his long white beard surely reached his navel.

To many, this would've been a frightening apparition, but the old man's ear-to-ear smile and obvious friendly nature put all fears to rest immediately.

"My name is Davol," the old Wizard said, "and we are about to become the best of friends."

At that point, Chedrick awakened.

CHAPTER 14—Parting is Such Sweet Sorrow

Awakening from his very real dream, Chedrick bolted from his sleeping pad. He staggered for a moment, having gotten up too quickly. From the sunlight beginning to brighten the morning sky, he realized that he had overslept substantially. Stumbling into the campfire's circle, Firefinger, with twinkling eyes, handed him a plate and asked with a smile, "You slept well?"

The words flowed out of Chedrick's mouth like water flowing in a small creek after a heavy rain. Tumbling together and roiling in their attempt to all get out at once, the words finally began making sense, as Chedrick described his wondrous dream to Firefinger.

Firefinger sat there holding his empty plate, grinning ear to ear, with a bemused look on his face, as Chedrick finally stopped for breath.

"I have somebody I want you to meet," Firefinger said.

It took a moment to register. Chedrick was so involved in telling the story of his dream, and his brain was so full of blue light and talking dragons that a moment slipped by before Firefinger's words registered.

At that instant, Chedrick became aware that somebody was standing behind him, and in that same instant, he felt a friendly, strong, warm hand on his right shoulder. Spinning his head to the right so fast he risked dizziness once more, he found himself looking up past the long white beard to the now familiar, friendly blue eyes of Davol loch Namor, the Wizard of his dream. Davol's eyes went beyond what most people consider "blue." It was almost as though they were illuminated from within–they had a subtle glow–and every once in a while, when Davol became passionate about something, tiny blue sparks could be seen flitting through the irises.

Chedrick turned and looked at Firefinger. He couldn't help but compare the two men. Firefinger was tall and strong. He exuded strength and confidence with his muscular body and tanned, rugged face. He turned back to look at the Wizard standing before him. Davol was half a head taller than Firefinger. He, too, exuded strength, and confidence, but in a far different way. There was an aura about him that immediately commanded respect. He was a large man. Not fat, not overtly muscular, just large. His long white beard nearly reached his beltline, and his thinning white hair cascaded down his back nearly as far. When he smiled, and he seemed to be constantly smiling, his blue eyes crinkled at the corners. When Chedrick looked into his eyes, he could feel the great depths of wisdom, compassion, and love within the Wizard.

Again, Chedrick found himself in the position of having so much to say that it couldn't get out of his mouth intact. His heart was full, but his mouth was empty.

Firefinger laughed aloud, a rare occurrence. Davol, as he made his way to Firefinger's side on the other side of the small fire pit, almost under his breath, gave a little chortle.

"That's it! That's exactly the sound the blue Dragon made!"

Davol and Firefinger looked at each other and burst into uproarious laughter, laughing together until tears flowed from their eyes. Chedrick just watched in stunned silence, his plate of food, now forgotten, slipped from his hand, and his mouth hung open.

"You're him! I mean, it's you! You're the one in my dream!" was all Chedrick was able to get out of his mouth. He continued to sit there, mouth agape, eyes wide, and totally befuddled.

"I suppose it's time we had a talk about this," Firefinger said.

"I have been aware since before the day I took you from your burning home who you were, what you are, and my purpose in your life. I cannot tell you who you are or what you are. That is for you to discover in your own way, and in your own time. If I were to tell you, I would be doing you a grave disservice. What you believe, you become. It is up to you to decide what it is that you believe.

I have known Davol most of my life. Indeed, he has been one of my greatest teachers. We had to wait until the works of the cosmos unfolded, and you grew into the man that you are before he could begin to be your teacher as well. The two of you are far closer than you might imagine. It is time now for you to leave my camp, to walk with Davol through strange lands and stranger times. Pay attention to all that you see, all that you hear, and especially all that you intuit. If I have taught you nothing else, it is my deep and abiding desire that I have taught you to pay attention to that which is unseen, but known, and to trust it. Therein lies the key to your future. Remember this always: the more you trust, the more you will be given to trust; the more you believe, the more you'll be given to believe. The hardest thing to learn to trust, and believe in, is your own abilities and achievements. You are far more than you have ever dared dream!"

"You have been a son to me," Firefinger said. "You have been more than a son to me. You will always have a place of honor in my heart, and I will never hear your name without feeling pride in the young man that you have become. But, for now, our time together is done. Go with Davol. Your future awaits you.

One more thing, son. This was wrapped with you in your blankets when I found you. You are to keep it with you at all times." Firefinger handed Chedrick a small leather drawstring pouch that held a clay disk as big as an English walnut, that held an image of a heart in a circle. "Keep this with you always, my son, and know, always, that I love you."

There were still tears flowing down Firefinger's craggy, tanned face, but no longer were they tears of laughter. They were now tears of pride, tears of joy, of loss, of celebration, and tears of love and separation.

For the rest of the day, the trio sat around the now cold fire and Chedrick listened, fascinated, as the two old friends relived astounding past adventures. As dusk began to show itself in the sky, the fire was rekindled from the coals, and Firefinger prepared dinner for all three.

As the last of the food was eaten, an extended silence fell over the small gathering, the kind of silence that says "This time is done. We have spoken all that we can speak about this for now. It is time for closure."

Davol stood up, his beautiful, sky-blue robes somehow unsullied by food or ash, and told Chedrick that he would come by just after sunrise in the morning and that Chedrick should pack only the most essential of his possessions for the unknown journey to come.

CHAPTER 15—We're Off to Be the Wizard!

It did not take long for Chedrick's world to spin on its axis. Just being near Davol was an electrifying experience. Even in daylight, when Davol stood against a dark background, sparks of bright vibrant blue light could be seen dancing near him. Birds and squirrels appeared not to fear him at all, and even the hulking bear they encountered seemed to respect his presence.

As they walked, Davol spoke of the nature of man, of nature, of time and space, and of the worlds beyond human knowledge, and the limitless nature of mankind.

Chedrick asked about divergent realities. Davol effortlessly manifested a length of chain such as a necklace might be made from. Holding the chain by one end, he began moving his hand in a tight circular motion. Almost immediately, the chain assumed a bow shape, bulging in the middle and tight at both ends.

"Observe, boy," the old Wizard began. "See how, in each moment, even though the top and the bottom of the chain remain almost stationary, there is an increasing difference away from the centerline in between those points. If you could stop the chain at one thousand points in its travels, you would find a thousand different realities for that chain. This is how different realities form from a common root. When you truly understand that all realities have commonalities, it becomes a simple matter to jump between them."

Time and again, Chedrick felt his eyes glaze over as the information overloaded his capacity for understanding. He felt as though he was being stretched beyond recognition by all this new knowledge. He soon began getting a severely dry mouth and a stabbing headache that felt like a hot nail had pierced his right eye straightaway through to the back of his skull. He did not mention a word about it to Davol, not daring to interrupt the flow of fascinating information.

Suddenly Davol stopped, turned to Chedrick, grasped him by the shoulders, and made eye contact. "Relax your body. You're suffering from an energy overload. That's what's giving you the headache and the dry mouth. Firefinger taught you how to ground yourself, but you neglected to practice your grounding techniques, and they are weak. Please allow me to show you what really good grounding feels like."

Davol stepped back a step, and with his right hand, he swept in a semi-circle to the right, bringing his palm to shoulder height in front of Chedrick. He then got a faraway look in his eyes and slowly, purposefully, brought his hand down, down, almost to knee level. As he did so, Chedrick felt his body simultaneously get heavier and heavier, relaxing as his mind quickly became quiet and alert. It almost felt as though he was going to sink slowly into the rich loam of the forest floor. At the same time, Chedrick realized that he had rarely felt so relaxed.

"THAT is what good grounding feels like, my boy."

With a start, Chedrick realized his mouth was no longer dry and that the headache was completely gone.

"What just happened?" Chedrick asked, astonished.

"When someone who is new to energy awareness of this level experiences large amounts of energy over an extended period of time, it can overload their system's ability to handle it gracefully. Dry mouth and that stabbing headache are common symptoms. From now on, you'll find that practicing grounding regularly will help you in many, many ways. Eventually, you will just BE grounded without having to think about it."

"But what exactly is grounding?" Chedrick asked. "I never really understood it."

Davol, sitting on a long-fallen log, reached down to the rich, brown earth at his feet and picked up a small branched twig only a couple of inches long. He rested his elbows on his knees and held an end of the twig in each hand, slowly turning it back and forth, examining the bark, and the texture of the broken ends. Finally, looking up, he dropped the twig and replied. "Every being consists of energy and many beings will wear a body. Of all the beings who wear bodies, only humans have forgotten that they are a part of the universal energy of life. Because of this, almost all humans give no thought whatsoever to their connectedness to all of life, to all of existence. Our beliefs and perceptions are powerful beyond measure, whether we understand that or not. Because we consider ourselves, as humans, to be alone as we walk through the universe, our energy reflects that. Instead of being an extension of all, we become walking bubbles of energy, disconnected and alone in the sea of life.

Grounding is consciously reconnecting to our source energy. It is accomplished by willing or allowing the earth and all other life energies to flow through us. It is a tremendously powerful balancing tool and can be used in countless ways, including ridding oneself of headaches, dry mouth, and other pains and ailments. You can accomplish what I just demonstrated to you, easily, for yourself. Close your eyes for a moment. And in your mind, to the best of your ability, allow yourself to feel your energy flow down and connect, in the heart of the earth, with all that is."

There was silence in the glade for several minutes as Chedrick followed the simple instructions and consciously connected his energy with the life forces of earth, the trees, the forest creatures, and Davol himself.

Slowly, gently, Chedrick pulled himself back out of the peaceful reverie of grounding, opened his eyes, looked at Davol, and smiled broadly.

"That was absolutely wonderful! And so easy! Thank you, my teacher. I shall be your follower from now on."

"Did you happen to notice how crystal-clear and unencumbered your mind became?" Davol asked. "That is a side effect of grounding, known as centering. It is releasing all unnecessary thoughts from your mind, leaving it clean and empty. Effective grounding and centering are the first steps toward meaningful and productive meditation. But that is enough for today.

When it comes to things of a Spiritual nature, you will

find that no matter what your question is, the answer is always 'It's simpler than that,'" Davol replied. "Simpler does not mean 'easier.' It means that it is less complicated than most people tend to make it. Always try to look past all the symptoms and complications the bushy foliage that surrounds any issue and go directly to the root of the issue or challenge. That is the simplest, and most direct and efficient method. And please, my boy, my name is Davol, and someday you will come to know that you are as much my teacher as I am yours. I can never be your leader. I can be your friend, your example, your confidant; I can be your guide. I can nudge you this way or that, but only you can determine your soul's path, and that is as it should be. The choices you make as you walk your road influence the remainder of your life, and, many times, the lives of those around you.

Choose wisely, my boy. Choose wisely in each moment and for each circumstance. You are your own leader, your own ultimate guide. There can be no other leader in your life. Chedrick, my boy, I neither seek nor accept 'followers.' I am your friend; a guide, a mentor, and nothing more. If you must put a label on our relationship, let it be that of brothers seeking answers. You can think of me as a helpful elder brother if you must.

There is one other ability that you will rarely use, though it can come in very handy. In a way, it's the opposite of grounding. Have you ever heard of levitation, boy?"

Davol shifted his body to a more comfortable position.

"Not that I recall, sir," Chedrick replied. "What is levitation?"

"See that apple tree over there?" Davol pointed with his chin towards a large apple tree growing amongst the oaks. Would you like an apple?"

Chedrick suddenly discovered that he was hungry and that apple sounded very good to him, but the lowest apple on the tree was well out of his reach.

"I'd love an apple, sir, would you like me to climb up and get one for you as well?"

Davol laughed a little laugh. "No, boy, I'll get them."

"But Davol, forgive me, you're an old man. I don't know that you should be climbing trees."

Davol threw back his head and roared with laughter. "Who said anything about climbing trees?"

He continued laughing as he strolled over closer to the tree. "You asked about levitation, boy?"

As he spoke, the Wizard slowly and effortlessly floated upward to where he could pick the apples which were now at his face level.

Once more, Chedrick's mouth hung open in disbelief. "What? How? How did you do that?"

Plucking two apples from the tree and descending slowly back to earth, Davol continued. "When the lightness of your Spirit overcomes the heaviness of your cares, you can fly. When the world tells you that it is impossible to do something, you are not required to believe them. That is one of the most important lessons I can ever teach you, Chedrick. Do not ever allow the limitations that others would place on you or the limitations you would place on yourself, mark the confines of your ability or effort. If you proceed through life believing that ALL things are possible, then nothing will be beyond your grasp. The more you believe, the more you will be given to believe, and the more you trust, the more you will be given to trust. When you learn to believe all and to trust all that you experience, you will truly become limitless, and miracles will be your everyday companion.

Now, I believe you wanted to talk about my homeland, Atlan."

Still stunned by what he had just witnessed and heard; Chedrick sat mutely as Davol continued.

"Always do that which seems 'right' at the moment. There is an important set of rules that every person of Atlan lives by: our planet first, our children second, our neighbor, third, and yourself, fourth, but never last. In following these guidelines, it is also important to consider your own value and your contribution and value to society. Do not needlessly endanger or waste the resource that is you, for that violates the first and second precepts. The philosophy is circular. You must care for yourself and your own needs so that you can care for the planet, the children, and your neighbor. Each is as important as the other."

CHAPTER 16—And Now for Something Completely Different

It was several months later, just as spring was touching the forest with green, that Davol and Chedrick were walking one morning when a Faerie suddenly appeared before Davol and engaged him in conversation. Like old friends, they spoke earnestly for several minutes, ignoring Chedrick completely.

Chedrick was dumbfounded. Like everyone, he had heard tales of the Faerie folk who were said to inhabit the forest, but, like everyone, he had dismissed the stories as being "old wife's tales."

In actuality, Faeries have been with us for tens of thousands of years. They are smart enough to stay out of sight of mankind and their flight is so swift that the human eye and mind simply do not perceive them while they are in flight. Thus, they are in effect, invisible. It is only when they stop traveling from place to place and hover or alight that they become visible to most humans. In fact, the collective term for a group of Faeries is "a Burst." Anyone who has ever witnessed a large group of Faeries arriving at a single location in a conflagration of sparkling wings and jewel tones, seemingly appearing magically from nothingness, will understand why they are called that. It is indeed a spectacular sight to behold.

Faeries are just over a foot tall, with shimmering, iridescent wings, thin limbs, and hard skin, like a beetle's. Their skin is a shimmering gold color with green highlights, with a slightly granular surface. They also have short green antennae with pear-shaped golden knobs at their ends. The antennae are very mobile and often seem to have a life of their own, becoming quite animated when a Faerie becomes excited.

The conversation finally wound down to the point that Davol could change the subject.

"Acorn, my friend, allow me to introduce Chedrick. Chedrick, this is my good friend Acorn. He's getting married in a fortnight, and we're both invited!"

Chedrick realized his mouth was once more agape, and that he probably looked pretty foolish to Acorn. He closed his mouth for a moment, then spoke. "A wedding? Faeries? A Faerie wedding! Let's go!"

Davol chuckled quietly. "We're going, boy. Faerie weddings don't happen often, and when they do, they are not to be missed!"

Faeries have their own language, of course, but Humans simply are not capable of speaking it, with all of its clicks, whistles, gutturals, and a strange silence that seems to suck all sound out of the air, tucked into the middle of a word. Not so much silence, but negative sound. That negative sound is as though a black hole opened in the middle of that word and sucked all of the sounds of the universe into it. It was that kind of a negative sound. For that reason, Humans and Faeries had been forced to agree on the use of common human words for Faeries' names.

Faeries are extremely long-lived, with an average lifespan of approximately 800 years. They were not considered to be completely adult until they reached the age of approximately 125 years. Some chose to form partnerships quite young in life, even at the young age of 85 years. Acorn was 143 years old. Chedrick was approaching 16 years on the human scale.

A juvenile Faerie is graced with wings sufficient for short flights among the trees in the meadows and could fly only slightly higher than the tallest trees. They are built very similarly to humans but not exactly. Valuing freedom as they do, it is no surprise that most Faeries did not encumber themselves with clothing for most occasions. Upon maturity and the selection of a mate, certain hormones were released that caused their wings to more than double in length, become iridescent, like jewels, and have a far greater capacity for flight and duration.

Much like a butterfly growing its wings out for when it leaves the cocoon; a Faerie's body would secrete additional fluids that inflated the juvenile wings into the glorious appendages of mature adulthood. This was most often triggered by a combination of excitement and hormones on the occasion of their conjugal flight, following an extended night of deep sleep, like a 15-hour hibernation.

On the morning of their bonding, the couple would appear in their newly enhanced and resplendent glory before the elders. Each wore only their wedding cloak. These were lavish affairs, the product of months of labor, embellished with threads of silver and gold, and accented with colorful gems. They covered from upper chest to mid-calf length, leaving cutaways for the wings, and were cleverly designed so that a single tug of the ornate knot at the top would release the entire garment, leaving the wearer completely sky-clad. Traditionally, simultaneously, each would release the cloak of their partner midway in the ascent flight, once they were out of view of those hovering below. As the cloaks fluttered back down to earth, it was considered great good luck to be the ones to catch them in mid-air. On the fifth anniversary of their flight, the cloaks would be gifted to the couple in another community ceremony.

***

The day of the ceremony began with a beautiful, warm, sunlit social time for all attendees. Chedrick and Davol mingled, eating Faerie delicacies and chatting with the other guests. Chedrick discovered to his dismay that some of the foods that the Faerie considered delicacies were not quite so palatable to the human tongue when he bit into a lovely morsel that held a candied grub within.

In the Faerie's sacred grove, the Matriarch stood before the assembled guests and the couple to be wed and recited the bonding ceremony:

"Family, Friends, and Fae
Let the celebration begin!
We are brought together today by hopes, by dreams, by the magic that is life itself.

Today, we celebrate the ascension of love, of hope, of laughter,
above tears, beyond fears.
The birth of commitment that spans many years.
Our gift of life begins as a seed, and in the heart of that seed,
we plant all things that we need
to learn, to grow, and to thrive.
To know the full meaning of being alive.

So now come ye, and gather around
And celebrate as these lives are bound
for as long as they will, as long as they may.
Be it forever, or be it a day.
Love has its preferences, and Fate has its way.

As both are willing, and as both commit
to building their altar to love
where they worship together, for the rest of their days.
That altar will see them grow strong and grow true,
will reward them and nurture them, leading their way
into their 'foreverness' after today.

That altar, their womb, from which will be born
all they can dream of,
dreams yet to be born.
Dreams may have brambles, that much is true,
but they also have blossoms to carry us through.
And in conquering brambles, they discover their strengths,
they discover their resources, they conquer new lengths
undreamt of.

And in that time when the dusk starts to fall,
and winter is coming, as it comes to us all,
may they wrap in their memories, drinking their tea
of what used to be 'you,' and used to be 'me,'
but has long since been 'us,' the sweetest of brews.
In front of a fireplace where brambles are burned,
and memories of flowers mark all that they've earned.

May all beings in the cosmos, may all forces of light,
bring blessings and joy to this couple tonight,
...and for each night together for as long as they choose.

Blessed be."

Then the couple leaps upward, using their fine, bejeweled wings for the first time as they climb skyward in unison. The sun catches the iridescent wings and sends a kaleidoscopic light show to all those watching below. The couple climbs out of sight, into the sky, and keeps flying straight up, until, finally, they simply can fly no higher.

When the magical flight reaches its uppermost point, the couple embrace, doing the things that Faeries do during a nuptial flight. Their wings, engorged by the tremendous exertion of the flight, stand stiffly out from their backs and act much like the fins on a maple seed, sending the united couple gently spiraling, twisting slowly, luxuriously, down from their heights as they leisurely and lovingly, complete their conjugal flight.

Just as they once again become visible to the villagers below, their wings rested from their long, languorous downward drifting journey, they both disappear in a blinding flash of wings, for several days of shared solitude before returning to their village and Faerie life. They fly off to a secret location that only their most trusted ally knows, a Faerie nest that has been stocked with all they need for their honeymoon. Once returned, in a week or so, the nuptial wings fall off, and are replaced by smaller adult wings, larger than the juvenile but still brightly jeweled transparent kaleidoscopes of color.

"But, isn't 800 years a long time to be married?" Chedrick asked.

Davol chuckled. "It is indeed, my boy," he replied. "The percentage of couples who stay together for an entire lifetime is very tiny indeed. As with all things human and Faerie, evolution and growth are always at work. As couples grow, there is always the chance that they will grow apart, and the perfect couple to-day, as they change and grow, may find that perfection slipping away over time. It would be extremely foolish and even destructive for them to stay in a relationship that has become toxic to them, or which no longer serves their joint growth.

Let me explain it to you this way."

CHAPTER 17—Union

"Beginning from the awareness that ALL things serve us in life, it must follow that ALL unions are classrooms for benefits and growth.

However, let us take the act of baking a cake as a good example of a union.

Perfect ingredients are provided to every baker; flawless, fresh, and wholesome. An experienced, professional baker knows what ingredients, what techniques, and what procedures, performed in the correct order, will result in a perfect cake.

But how boring to produce perfect cakes that are all the same. Souls need experiences, variety, and self-exploration to continue their growth process!

Free will enters the picture.

Bakers with little or no skills or experience will produce a wild variety of baked goods, ranging from a total disaster to an exquisite, one might even say, flawless, cake.

Experienced, well-educated, and seasoned bakers may choose to 'tweak' this and 'tweak' that, to try different variations of their tried-and-true recipe to find a different, also flawless, variation on their recipe.

Then there are those who over-think the process, getting frozen into the 'what-if's' and the 'yes, but's' of the process and never actually get around to turning on their ovens.

Guess what! There is an infinite supply of perfect ingredients.

Experiment! Grow!

Try new and different things.

If one recipe doesn't work out to your liking, change it a little or a lot and give it another try. You have countless lifetimes to 'get it right,' and every attempt makes you a better baker!"

Chedrick thought for a moment, his face scrunched up

in a bit of a frown creasing his brow. “So, forever doesn’t always mean forever?”

“Forever means, in that moment, that there is every intention of living out your life with that partner. As life happens and years pass, partners can and should grow and change. Sometimes they grow together, and other times they grow apart, but in the beginning, the intention is for a ‘forever’ relationship.”

***

The next morning was heavy with the rain that had been falling all night. Chedrick awoke, full of wonder. For a change, he awoke even before Davol.

“Davol! Davol! I had the most incredible dream this morning. I felt like it was real!”

Davol cracked open one eyelid and looked at his student with a slight smile. “So, tell me about it, my boy.”

Chedrick’s eyes took on a faraway look as he re-entered the magical world of his dream. It was SO real! His voice changed slightly, due to his altered state of consciousness. He began his recitation of the lesson…

“I found myself on a misty, magical, moonlit mountainside.

There is a mossy, ancient, weathered, oaken bucket that sits slightly askew on a moss-covered rock, limned in moonlight.

The class began.

The nature of magic, the substance of spells,” is the subject. “Our teacher was a tall man in a blue robe with long white hair and a long white beard. He looked much like you. He even had your blue eyes, but he looked much younger.”

Chedrick glanced toward his mentor, but Davol had closed his eye while listening. Davol lifted his hand and waggled a finger in a circle, signing that Chedrick should continue his story.

“A richly jeweled trifle, an artifact of intense beauty, shimmering with rich blues, golds, reds, and greens as feathers turned to threads and threads turned to light it was a shimmering swirl of colors with multicolored fire everywhere. This object of beauty was suspended before my eyes in the light and rotated slowly so that I could fully appreciate the beauty and intricacy of its construction. It seemed to be a combination of sculpture, of a weaver's finest work, and a jeweler's greatest pride.

This, I was told, is the visual image of a spell.

This glowing artifact was then submerged slowly into the oaken bucket, into a liquid known as the 'remover of illusions,' so that I might learn more about how it is made.

As it descended into the liquid, the colors, the threads, the feathers, the sparkles all fall away and dissolve. They disappear and cease to exist. All that is left are loosely intertwined threads of various thicknesses of what appeared to be silver but was not.

My curiosity asked, 'What is this matter?' and the answer came within the vision.

A new vessel appeared. It was ancient stone. A depression capable of holding a large melon was carved in the top, but the vessel was empty.

I was shown without seeing, taught without words. Knowingness was my tutor.

I observed as a fine, gentle, nearly invisible, mist filled the cup in the ancient stone. I was aware that this mist was 'highest intent' made manifest. As the moon shone down upon it, each strand of the mist was embraced, enfolded, and entwined in the silver moonlight. As the strands were gently embraced, they intertwined with one another, creating the interlacing structures that I saw when the spell was first dissolved by the 'remover of illusions.'

I am aware now, that this is the heart of every spell. Pure intentions, wrapped in moonlight and reinforced by its silver strands.

I learned all of this in an instant.

The focus, the intent of the practitioner, builds on the silver structure, and dresses this framework of highest intent in the finery that will be its final form as it is sent out into the world.

Then the dream faded away, and I awakened with a poem in my head. I wanted to share all this with you before I forgot it. Here's the poem."

Birth of Spells

"Highest intentions
Invisible mist
Laid out in moonlight
With Argent, they're kissed
Cradled, not captured
In swaddling of light
They stand at the ready,
For soon, they take flight."

Davol chuckled softly. "That was no dream, my boy. You're attending class in the ethers in your dream time. When our conscious mind is asleep, it makes it far easier for some people to grasp what is being offered by the Spirit realm. There are many qualified teachers available to teach you during your dream time. You will know when you are being taught by the strength of the dream and the extreme details of the experience. Pay close attention to dreams such as these, for they will teach you for all of your life if you are open to them."

CHAPTER 18—How the Faerie Came to Earth

In the early Fall of that year, while in a remote and beautiful meadow grove near a small brook of clean water that seemed to be talking to itself as it tumbled over the rounded stones of its bed, the sounds of a nearby conversation caused Chedrick to stir from his deep slumber. Raising his head and opening his eyes, he discovered Davol and Acorn sitting near the small fire pit, where a newly freshened supply of kindling was just beginning to catch. It was a brisk morning, and the Wizard and the Faerie sat close to the tiny flames, rubbing their hands and holding them out to catch the warmth of the fire.

Both knew the instant the Chedrick awakened but continued their conversation in low tones.

"Tell me more about your Atlan. Teacher's Park is such a beautiful place. And Leahndreal! All those beings, all those races! Even though you took me there and showed it to me, I still find it hard to believe." Acorn shook his head in wonder.

By now, Chedrick was wide awake and all ears.

Throwing his sleeping robe off, and sitting bolt upright, he asked with a voice a little too loud, "Atlan? Teacher's Park? Leahndreal? What are these places? Can you take me there too?"

"Well, well. Look who has finally decided to join us this morning. Acorn and I were just talking about the history of the Faerie on earth.

Many years ago, he had asked me whether the Faerie teachings were true, that the Faerie did not originate on Earth, but arrived from a different reality when many other races were establishing colonies, during the first Golden age of Atlan. I took him through space and time and across several realities, so that he could see for himself that they were indeed true."

Dumbfounded, Chedrick shook his head. "Say that again, please?"

"I believe that I have explained to you before, boy, that the world you see around you is not the only version of our world to exist.

If, for instance, you had awakened earlier this morning, you would've heard more of our conversation, and we would not need to be having the conversation that we are having now. You would have created another timeline through your choices and actions. Every time we take an action, there are alternate actions that could have been taken; alternate results that would have followed, and an alternate, slightly different reality is born in every moment by every action of every being.

These realities travel through time in a mostly parallel path to one another, with a few radical exceptions. When we truly understand time and space, and energetic BEingness, it becomes very easy to simply step sideways from our path to another path, and another, and another, until we get to the path we wish to explore. Eventually, we learn to step directly to the reality we seek without having to pass through others.

Millennia in the past, the Faerie folk, for their own reasons, created a small colony on earth. Due to unpleasant circumstances on their home world, they, as a group, sidestepped into this reality that we now share.

It was in the time of the Long-Ago, in the Before. It was before the great darkness of war and ignorance, the time of a thoughtless quest for power when greed enveloped the Earth and the glories of hundreds of thousands of years of an advanced civilization were lost in a day. That civilization was one of innovative science and art, of prosperity and universal peace. It was the time of Atlan, and of Leahndreal," Davol continued.

"What is an 'Atlan,' and a 'Leahndreal?'" Chedrick asked. "You took him through time?!?"

The old Wizard looked at the boy. "The more you trust, the more you will be given to trust, and the more you believe, the more you will be given to believe. Your mind is your most powerful tool."

Acorn looked at Davol with questions in his eyes, and, when Davol nodded slightly, Acorn spoke.

Acorn settled himself on a moss-covered stump near Chedrick and began his tale.

"The Faerie is a very ancient race with a very long history on their own planet and others, including this one. We are peaceful forest dwellers and we live on what the forest provides, in harmony with all other beings. We first came to your planet over a million years ago and settled in your forests. After about half a million years, there was a tremendous increase in volcanic activity on our home planet, following an asteroid strike, and the toxic clouds of gas and the tremendous mountains of ash buried our forests and made life unlivable for us. We sent scouts to look at other planets and realities, and settled on the reality that your people call Earth.

As a group, we made the shift from our old reality stream to the one that you occupy, and here we are today, having this conversation, a conversation that never would have occurred otherwise.

About 200,000 years ago, refugees from the sunken continent of Lemuria, who had settled in Atlan, sent emissaries to our land in the North, which we had named for our first Queen, Leahandra. We welcomed them to our land.

In the days of Before, when this world was far different from the one we find ourselves in today, peace, cooperation, and prosperity were the norms. With our permission, the Atlanteans and the Star Brothers built a trans-dimensional hub near one of our forests to facilitate travel between the stars and dimensions. It eventually became the second largest community on the planet, second only to Atlan's capital city, also called Atlan.

Atlan had guided the world to a place of harmonic cooperation for the benefit of all. Its colonies could be found on every continent and were invariably centers of science, the arts, and commerce. The hub, in our rich and verdant northern land, became a crossroads for space and time travelers from this planet and others, even for other dimensions and reality streams. To visit Leahndreal was to see the entire cosmos. Beings and cultures undreamt of to the ordinary man were commonplace there.

Powered by the Atlantean power grid, it served as Earth's gateway to and from the stars and different dimensions.

Because of the deep and long-standing association between our respected Star Brothers and the Atlantean civilization, many off-world societies and governments sent ambassadors, teachers, scholars, and artists to earth, to Atlan, for mutual benefit and shared learning opportunities."

"Wait! Wait!" Chedrick, unable to contain himself, jumped up off the log he had been sitting on and stood directly in front of Acorn, towering over the tiny Faerie. "What are you talking about? Atlan? Star Brothers? Leahndreal? Dimensions?"

There was a quiet chuckle, not quite a chortle, but close, that came from behind Chedrick. "Sit down, my boy; sit down. This is a very long story and we've only just begun to tell it. Be patient and pay attention and all your questions will be answered."

Sheepishly, Chedrick backed up, retracing the four steps to where he had been sitting, glanced quickly behind him to make sure he was positioned correctly, and resumed his previous place on the log.

"Atlan is the land of my birth," Davol continued. "It was a land, a society, which had been in existence for nearly 320,000 years at the time of my birth, and for 20,000 years after it. With the help and guidance of our Star Brothers, we had achieved a stable, abundant, compassionate society that far surpassed all other earthly civilizations of the time. We will speak much more about Atlan in the future. In fact, I intend to take you there."

This, of course, triggered another cascade of questions in Chedrick's mind, but Chedrick was a fast learner and he kept his mouth shut, understanding that this was a time for listening.

Acorn continued his story. "On our home planet of G|bo*sh, there are three species which could be considered sentient beings. Ours is a water world with four widely separated continents and a smattering of islands. Two of these species evolved on widely separated continents and remain at a rather primitive level even today.

"Because we evolved sooner than the other species,

our Faerie council set aside the separate continents where they evolved as their own lands, never to be encroached upon by the Faerie. The other species were the Ca'al, an iridescent-plumed, flightless avian species whose wings have evolved into six-fingered hands, and the Areta, resembling fat, fuzzy, three-foot caterpillars. Their top three sets of legs are foot-long tentacles with three smaller, dexterous, and highly sensitive tentacles at the tip of each of those arms. They have become very good at creating intricate artistic works that are traded across the universe. These both are native to our planet but completely different from us. We were originally insects, but we developed a high level of language, science, and culture far earlier than the other races. We had the opportunity to exercise greed to wipe them out and take over their territories as our own or enslave them; but because of the Star Brothers and their teaching of The Way, we set aside their continents to be theirs forever, that they might continue to evolve in their own time and their own way without interference. Instead of expanding on our own planet, we chose to explore space, time, and multiple dimensions in search of additional planets where we might begin colonies without causing harm to any native species.

"Leahndreal became one of the major hubs for such travel, and Atlan was recognized as one of the foremost centers of civilization in this quadrant. It was not unusual, on any given day in Leahndreal, to see beings representing several races of giants, Mer people, Selkie, Gnomes, Centaurs and Unicorns, Star Brothers, and, of course, Faerie folk, among others. There was a constant flow of Travelers from all corners of the universes, and many races were represented by large enclaves or even small communities of their own people.

"On that terrible, terrible day when Atlan fell, the entire power grid of this planet fell with it. The Galactic Senate immediately declared Earth to be off-limits, and all trade, communication, and travel were banned. Those who were living here had no choice or option to return to their planet of origin.

"For many, many generations, chaos reigned. Madness had come to this world, and no one was safe, especially those who looked or seemed different. Species after species were hunted down and eliminated until we finally learned that we could not openly walk this world or be seen by Man. We went into hiding in order to survive. The Mers and the Selky retreated to the seas, while the centaurs sought the plains, and the forest folk, the Faerie, the Dryads, the Nymphs, the Ents, and many of the giants found refuge in the woods. Life was very difficult for many, and some species perished entirely. The Faerie folk were very fortunate. Your forests on earth are very similar to those of our home planet, and we easily adapted to them and have done well here."

CHAPTER 19—Auntie Ent

As Acorn spoke, Chedrick kept feeling as though they were being observed by someone close by. He kept hearing leaves moving and rustling but there was no breeze, and he was unable to see any other cause for the noise.

Suddenly, in what seemed to be a very loud whisper coming from everywhere at once, and no place in particular, he heard a slightly raspy, genderless voice say, "That was pretty accurate, as far as it goes, but there is more…"

Chedrick's head spun this way and that as he tried to identify the source of that voice, but to no avail. Confusing him further, Davol and Acorn were acting as though nothing out of the ordinary had happened.

The dry voice continued, "Allow me pleased to introduce myself. I am The Historian, but you may call me Auntie Ent. That's what all my friends call me."

Thoroughly confused by now, Chedrick bounded from his sitting position, tripping over a stick in the process, and barely catching his balance before falling. "Who are you? Where are you? What are you? I don't see you anywhere!"

Davol chortled, Acorn tittered, and the sound of dry laughter filled the air. "I'm right here. Right in front of you! If you take a couple of steps forward and reach out your hand, you'll touch me!"

Chedrick continued looking wildly around himself, trying to find the speaker. Finally, Davol chuckled and said, "Follow her instructions, lad."

Feeling very foolish, and suspecting that a joke was being played on him, Chedrick took two steps forward. The only thing in front of him was the trunk of a very large, very ancient tree. It was not a variety that he had seen before in all of his years in the woods.

"Touch her!" Davol said.

"Touch who?" Chedrick replied. "I don't see anybody. Whom am I supposed to touch?"

"Touch the tree," Acorn said. "Touch the tree! The tree is The Historian! Auntie Ent!"

Auntie Ent was the last of the Ent tribe on earth Her mother had been a Matriarch. Much like a queen bee, Auntie Ent's mother was the only Ent capable of producing viable seedlings and had just arrived on Earth as a young ambassador/advisor to Atlan when The Collapse occurred.

Like all Ents, the Matriarch had a long, long lifetime, measured in thousands of years. Very late in her life, the Matriarch produced one last, small, crop of viable seeds, and, as there were very few living Ents to plant and nourish them, gave them over to the Faerie folk to protect and plant. Ents are solitary beings and do not mind living their long lives alone, contemplating life and the universe as their toes grow ever longer into the soil. In fact, the Faerie word for Ent translates to "Long toes." There had always been a special bond between the Ents and the Faerie, as both had deep ties to the forest, the soil, the plant kingdom, and nature.

Ents are able, with some difficulty, to change locations in their youth, but after about 2500 years of age, they usually will pick a location that they find both beautiful and safe, and settle in that spot for the rest of their lives.

Ents have very sharp memories, rich in the detail gleaned through ages of unhurried observation, and passed from Ent generation to Ent generation. This is why they were often addressed in direct formal conversation as "Dear Historian."

Because the Faerie folk had such high regard for the Ents, they planted only one seed every two thousand years, in carefully chosen and isolated areas, far from the eyes of Man. Men correctly thought that the wood from an Ent had special, magical properties, and often would chop one to splinters for profit when an Ent was discovered. Davol's knotted, blonde wooden staff, it is said, was created from a branch of Ent wood, grown especially for him and gifted to him by the Ents in a rare sign of respect and gratitude.

When the time came to plant the last Ent seed, there was a solemn, bittersweet ceremony, for this would be the last Ent ever to be seen on earth. That was nearly 3,000 years ago, and Auntie was that final Ent. Now a 'long toes,' indeed, she had chosen to live in the deep, deep forest in a peaceful, verdant river valley rarely visited by Man.

Hesitantly, Chedrick reached out and touched the tree's bark. Immediately, the voice lost its raspy tone and rang clearly inside his head. The rustling of the leaves had ceased. Chedrick now heard not only her words but was aware of everything that went into her selection of those words.

Startled, he drew his hand back rapidly, but the conversation continued in his head.

"Now that we have connected, I will be able to speak with you more easily and communicate with you far more clearly."

"How can I continue to hear you in my head?" Chedrick asked. "What's happening?"

Davol stepped up to the boy and put his arm around Chedrick's shoulders. "Remember the times that you knew that Firefinger wanted you to come to him, and you found him easily, even though he was in a part of the woods you had never been in before?"

"Yes, of course," Chedrick replied.

"Did you ever wonder how that happened?"

"Father told me we were practicing something called tele… tele… something."

"Telepathy, my boy! Telepathy. Telepathy is sending words, pictures, and thoughts directly from your mind to the mind of someone else. Language and translation are never a problem because each mind receives the thoughts in its own language. It is the purest form of communication known." Davol continued. "Ents are telepathic creatures. When Ents choose to speak aloud to Man, their voices sound like a breeze rustling leaves as it passes, because, well, the Ents have learned to speak Man's languages by rustling their leaves in a particular way. Ents speak aloud by carefully selecting leaves and twigs of a certain size and causing them to rustle together in a specific way that results in a surprisingly good approximation of human speech. Large leaves produce the base notes and small leaves and twigs the high and medium notes, but the Ent's natural form of communication is telepathy.

Unfortunately, untrained humans can only pick this up at a very short range. Well-meaning humans whom the Ents have learned, over time, to trust, have found that they 'heard' better if they embraced the tree, or sat between its roots, and others have developed the rather annoying habit of knocking on the trunk to wake up the Spirit of the tree within.

Because you are who you are, and because of the training that you have received from your father, your ability to communicate telepathically is significantly better than the average human. When you touched Auntie Ent's skin, you completed a connection that your brain will recognize for the rest of your life. Now you will be able to communicate, no matter where, or when, you are, and the more often you connect and communicate the easier and the clearer that communication will be."

"Now that we have that out of the way," the clear voice in his head said, "may I continue with the story of how the Faerie folk came to be on earth?" Historians had the unfortunate habit of wanting to share all their knowledge on a particular subject whenever asked about it. Because time meant next to nothing to them, they sometimes forgot that, for those with considerably shorter lifespans, a three-week-long explanation could be a real burden.

"Briefly, my friend," Davol replied with a broad smile. He had been through many of Auntie Ent's lectures. Four and a half hours later, Auntie Ent had reached the point in her, to her point of view, very abbreviated story wherein the Faerie folk had established a vibrant community near Leahndreal, 312,500 years before The Collapse. Davol gave an exaggerated stretch, and said, "Well, dear Auntie, it's time for the mortals among us to get some sleep." He glanced knowingly at Chedrick's nodding head and glazed-over eyes. Acorn was also showing signs of impending sleep.

Bowing his head ever so slightly, Davol assumed a formal stance and said "Thank you, Dear Historian, for sharing your knowledge with us. In return, we offer respect and gratitude."

The only payment Ents understood or accepted was an acknowledgment that that which they had offered had value to the recipient. The verbal offering of respect reflected the ancient, unspoken agreement between the Ents and other races. Ents would freely, even gladly, share information, but only so long as there was genuine gratitude and respect offered in return.

CHAPTER 20—Limitless

One frosty morning, as they were walking through the woods in silence, each one meditating on their own thoughts, Chedrick suddenly broke the silence. Turning to Davol, he asked, "How old ARE you, Davol?"

Davol's ancient face crinkled into a huge smile, his eyes sparkling with mischievous delight. "Like you, my boy, I am more ancient than time itself. I have been in existence since before there was existence. I will be in existence when the worlds have turned to dust, and that dust, to nothingness."

Confused, Chedrick restated his question.

Laughing, eyes still sparkling, Davol replied, "Oh, you mean in THIS body! My soul has existed in this body for almost 800 years. I still have quite a few years to go in this body before it is time for me to dissolve into the mists of Avalon."

By now thoroughly confused, Chedrick had a million questions, but could only ask them one at a time.

"How many bodies do you have, Davol? You've been alive for almost 800 years? What are the mists of Avalon?"

Laughing compassionately, Davol answered these questions in order.

"We all wear many, many bodies over many, many lifetimes. We are eternal, but the bodies we wear are not. When one body reaches its end, it is time to lay it down and, when it is right to do so, don another. Our essence remains the same, even though we often change from male to female, from one culture to another, from one time to another, even one reality to another. Although some recall some aspects of their prior existence, most do not, as each lifetime brings its own unique challenges and goals, its own tools and lessons. Clarity of mind and purpose are necessary to successfully complete those goals. Having carryover memories of other lifetimes and challenges only complicates things for most.

This universe we live in, my boy, is far, far more than what you see, what you hear, what you feel, and what you think.

The universe is not limited by our limitations or the limits of our perceptions, but the personal limitations we accept are the brushes that we use to paint the picture we hold in our minds of what the universe is.

Our universe is said to be limitless. Something without limits is also called infinite. Both of these terms simply mean that it is beyond our ability to imagine or comprehend. It also means that ALL things are not only possible, but they have already happened countless times."

"Once we realize, understand, and accept the infinite nature of our reality and ourselves, we can set aside our beliefs regarding our limitations, and begin to act as the limitless beings that we are. All things are possible to those who believe that they are possible.

I was born a very long time ago in a land that no longer exists, in a culture that was torn from this world. I have traveled through what mankind calls time, and across several realities, to be here with you today.

In my youth it was not uncommon to occasionally see our Star Brothers speaking to a crowd or simply walking down the paths in our city. They were very easy to see because of their height, but otherwise, they looked very much like us. When I was still quite young, because of my elevated lineage, which includes noble star blood, I was selected to travel to their planet, where I was educated for 35 years before returning to this planet. I have learned many things above and beyond what was available to the common person. Some of those things have enabled me to live far beyond the normal lifespan, which was, in Atlan, in my time, 180 to 200 years. People were not considered to be adults until they reached their mid-50s, and old age began at about 150 years.

As for dissolving in the mists of Avalon, when the time comes, you will understand."

"What do you mean 'we have many bodies?' I only have this ONE!"

"Sit down, boy. This may take a while…"

CHAPTER 21—Lifting the Veil

Davol settled down gently on an ancient, moss-covered log that was beginning to soften and sag in places. It looked to be comfortable for a long sit down and chat.

"In the years that you spent with your father, Firefinger, you saw him do many things that the common folk would say were impossible. He taught you to do many of these things yourself. Is that not correct?"

Chedrick nodded in agreement. "Yes, I do have many uncommon skills that Firefinger taught me."

Davol continued. "Did you ever wonder why the skills are uncommon?"

"No. It never came to mind. It was just the way we did things."

"In more enlightened times, every person had every skill that you have seen Firefinger use, every gift you have seen me use, and more. Those who sought to have controlling powers in this world determined that their power would be easier to keep and wield against a populace who thought they were powerless.

Over a long period of time, the common folk were taught to fear and hate their own energetic abilities, gifts, and powers. Because these gifts were no longer spoken of or taught, they have died out in the world, with only a spark of light here and there. You, Firefinger, and I are carriers of that spark. We are the ones whose job it is to fan it, keep it alive, and pass it on to others, so that it may live in this world of darkness until it is time for our light to burst forth again into the world."

Davol paused for a moment, a faraway look in his eyes. He watched a squirrel playing in the trees for a moment. "It is time."

"Time for what?" Chedrick asked.

"It is time for the next level of your education," Davol replied. "You asked about our many bodies. I want to show you some things. The first step in discovering your true self lies in rejecting who you have been trained to think you are.

One of the abilities that I have not yet shown you involves

traveling across time, space, realities, and dimensions. All of these things are illusions to those who comprehend and follow The Way. Once one recognizes that they are an illusion, they no longer exist as barriers, and can easily be traversed energetically and physically."

"I don't understand." Chedrick looked confused.

"Here's a simple, basic explanation. If we were to set out to walk to the village we passed through yesterday, how long would it take us to arrive?"

Chedrick thought for a second. "The same time it took us to walk from there to here. Most of a day."

"Now, if I asked you to revisit that village in your mind, how long would it take you to go there?" Davol asked.

"No time. I'm already there, in my mind." Chedrick replied.

"Exactly!" Davol said. "That is the principle that we will use for our travels."

BOOK TWO—TRAVELERS…

Episode 1—A Visit to Atlan

Davol came strolling back into camp just before midday one day, in conversation with a half-dozen Faeries circling around his head. As they neared Chedrick, the Faeries disappeared in a blur of motion and a sparkle of bejeweled wings.

Davol seated himself on a favorite stump. It seemed to have been shaped to especially fit him, with a deeply moss-covered hollow to sit upon, weathered, mossy rims on either side like an overstuffed chair, and a comfortable, tall back. It was almost as though nature had created a throne for him.

"Acorn is going to be a father!" Davol proclaimed.

"That's wonderful! I'm so very happy for him! Can we go visit him?"

"Perhaps later, my boy. The hatching is still far in the future. There will be time enough later."

Faeries, of course, have evolved from insects, so the birth of a Faerie involves a prolonged larval stage, then more time as a pupa. The entire process requires slightly longer than two and one-half years. The pupa is placed into a special cavity in the father's carapace, on his back, and under his left wing, and then a thin film of chitinous material forms over the cavity and hardens in order to protect the child as it develops for the next two years. When the child completes its growth into a young Faerie, the covering falls away and the young Faerie emerges into the world. A great celebration is held when it is time for the hard chitinous film to rupture and the fledgling Faerie to burst forth.

Because of their long life span, Faeries did not often have offspring.

Davol changed the subject. "Now, before we begin our journeys, there are some things that I would like to tell you.

Because Atlan was in a temperate climate, minimal protective clothing was needed, and we were not a modest people. Atlantean culture has long accepted the human form as beautiful. Aspects of the human body have not been sexualized, and it is very common to see partial or full nudity on the streets of Atlan. Because it is so commonplace, it is easily and readily accepted with comfort by all genders. Both men and women often went about with exposed chests, and a commonly seen garb was the gauzy fabric skirts that ended just above the knee. These were known as 'kruts,' and were generally seen in muted earth tones, though sometimes with fancy embroidery. For festive celebrations, bright, colorful kruts with geometric designs were often worn. Occasionally, for more formal gatherings, a loose-fitting gown that hung from a single shoulder, known as an 'andikrut' would be worn. Some citizens also chose to wear sandals, called 'tuks,' though most opted for bare feet.

Earth is far from being the only planet that ever has, or will, support life, and life can take many different forms. Sometimes, those forms are not what one would expect. The travels we are about to undertake will demonstrate that clearly to you.

As an example, the very first time I came to earth was as a rock. To be more precise, I was a mountain-sized mass of granite floating in a molten lake of magma within the newly formed Earth, which was only two-thirds the size of the planet that you live on today."

***

Over the next few months, Davol undertook to educate Chedrick in the arts of the Traveler.

"A Traveler is one who moves freely through time and space, and only the greatest of adepts will sense his presence. A Traveler is someone who can consciously choose to visit other times, places, and realities without taking their body with them. A Traveler is present, but not part of, that which he or she observes. A Traveler cannot be seen or heard by those he is visiting. A Traveler is a student, an observer. A Traveler can see, but can only very rarely be perceived by those he observes. A

Traveler can hear but is almost never heard. While it is possible for the most advanced Travelers to interact in the environment they visit, it is usually recommended not to do so.

Remember that we are visitors and observers only. There is nothing we can do to affect or change that which we observe. The conditions, places, people, and events that we will see may shock or surprise you. It is their world, not ours. What you will see is perfectly natural and in order at each time and place. We cannot interact with those that we observe, and with only extremely rare exceptions, they will be completely unaware of our presence.

I believe you're finally ready, my boy," the Wizard proclaimed one spring afternoon. "You now have a pretty good idea of what to expect as a Traveler, and what is expected of you. There are, of course, ways and methods to Travel physically and manifest physically in different realms and times, but there are rules and there can be serious consequences when those rules are broken. When the time is right, you will learn how to Travel physically, but that time is not today. Remember always, the one cardinal rule of physical Traveling is to never, ever, under any circumstances, meet yourself in the physical. As with all rules, there can be exceptions, but only in exceptional circumstances. As you learn more, you will understand that better.

Before we go, though, I would like you to read this." Davol gives Chedrick a thin book from the distant future. On the cover is emblazoned the title, "A Traveler's Guide to Old Atlan."

Unlike the weighty vellum volumes Chedrick had seen before, this one was made of thin sheets of paper, all the same size, and the letters were written by some process that made them very easy to read, unlike the handwritten pages he had seen before. It had stiff paper covers and was much lighter than any other book he'd ever held.

"I would like for you to read this tonight, my boy. Tomorrow, we Travel.

For our first journey, I will take you to my homeland of

Atlan, and give you a tour of my daily life there."

By now quite proficient in reading, Chedrick devoured the book in a couple of hours while Davol waited patiently.

The book contained a brief outline of the highlights and foundations of the life and times of this planet's highest civilization as it existed nearly 30,000 years ago. At the time of Davol's birth, Atlan was almost 8,000 years into its second and final "Golden Age."

The book discussed the societal structure and existence of the Nation-State of Atlan, without consideration for contemporary social, political and religious constraints. The book spoke of Atlantean life simply "as it was." The social and political patterns of old Atlan did not appear overnight but were the product of careful planning and thoughtful, benign guidance over a long period. Once achieved, they became self-sustaining; nurturing the nation and the world.

The civilization the world refers to as 'Atlantis' had existed for over 300 millennia and eventually maintained outposts and colonies. Those outposts included settlements scattered all over this planet. Some were in Egypt, the Himalayas, Lake Titicaca in Peru, and in a forgotten land named Leahndreal, which is called Ireland today,

The philosophy of old Atlan can be accurately stated in a single word: "Mindfulness." From infancy on, every citizen of Atlan was trained and encouraged to consider the wants, needs, and comfort of their neighbors as equal to or above their own. The city-state of Atlan could have been considered an organism. The communities and social groups were the organs of the organism and each individual was a cell. None could survive without the others.

The education of the populace the children, in particular, was of the highest importance, but the Atlantean educational system bore little resemblance to that of today's world, as the book said. Each individual was encouraged to pursue wherever their interests lead them, with guidance from more experienced individuals in the same or related fields. As a result, Atlantean adults made art, grew gardens, and did research in the fields they loved most.

The Atlantean term for education is best translated as "opening the eye." In a society such as Atlan, the maturity of the society, combined with the science and support of the Star Brothers and their technology, ensured that no one wanted for anything. This provided tremendous freedom of expression for the populace. Those who were interested in the arts could pursue any form of art they wished, while those who were drawn inexorably to studying the hormone cycles in ice worms were allowed to immerse themselves in the studies that they loved. Some thrived on creating the beautiful gardens and parks of Atlan. Thus, everyone had a job that they loved, that they could work at as little or as devotedly as they chose for their entire life, without worrying about paying bills, or even money, for that matter.

There was no such thing as money, as the Atlanteans had a gift-based society. People did what they loved because they loved it, and freely gifted the proceeds of their labor to individuals or to society as a whole. Everyone was guaranteed their basic needs, and those who gave more received more from the community in return.

It was said in Atlan that "nurturing our children's minds and Spirits is like 'giving royal jelly to a bee.'" Everything in Atlan revolved around the concept of a strong and vibrant future. It was said to "consider first the grandchildren, next the children, and last yourself." Atlan had a society built on "How can I help you?" not "How can I get more for myself."

When an entire civilization operates on this premise, all benefit, and none suffer.

Atlan's system of government is best described as a democratic meritocracy, wherein those who were recognized as the most dedicated and effective servants of the land were honored and elevated to a position on the High Council if they so desired. Those who had served on the High Council for a period of 75 years were eligible to be elevated to the Council Emeritus, and the High Council and the Council Emeritus together were called the Grand Council. All issues were settled by consensus, with the Council Emeritus being given a single vote equivalent to 25% of the total. There was also the Council of Advisors, the general counsel. These were those who have not quite earned a position on the Council itself but were being considered and trained for that position.

The Atlanteans had no religion. Rather, they had a belief system focused on the most important Trinity: environment, society, and self, in that order. The sanctity and scope of the human spirit was their guiding force. Their rules in everyday life were based in mindfulness. To be honest, to help others, and to be kind. Their belief system was called simply "The Way," and it went far beyond the physical. It encompassed Spiritual beliefs and understanding as well.

The symbol that the Atlanteans had adopted to represent the way was the very symbol embossed on the ancient clay disk Chedrick carried in a pouch around his neck. The symbol was a circle with a small opening at the top. Contained within the circle was a heart shape, with small openings at the top and bottom.

Davol, looking over Chedrick's shoulder as he read, interjected with further details.

"The heart shape represents that which we refer to as 'life.' We enter the small opening at the top, in the process we call birth. During that time, our conscious minds have the greatest natural connection to Spirit. As we travel through life, our interests become more and more focused, and one of our main purposes is to overcome the illusion of separation from Spirit and one another. In an ideal life, we completely overcome that illusion until, completely focused on the unity of all things, we exit life from that exit point at the bottom of the heart shape, in a process called 'death,' and we return to 'All That Is,' the space within the circle.

Returning to all that is, we resume our oneness with all that is. There is no place, there is no time, there only is, IS. Eventually, we make the choice to return to a body in the act referred to as 'reincarnation' and begin the process anew in order to further refine our spirit.

The condition of oneness outside the body, as described by the large circle, includes everything the mind of Man might possibly conceive.

But there is a hole at the top of the circle, and that opening connects to that which the mind of Man might never conceive.

Every belief system has some truth. None, including The Way, has all of it. That is the space beyond the circle that no living mind can envision or hope to comprehend. We are that, also.

That, dear boy, is the meaning of the symbol that you wear around your neck."

All life was respected by the Atlanteans, and existence itself was both sacred to them and a manifestation of that sacred nature.

Founded over 3,000 centuries before by the last remaining survivors of the Moria people from the far more ancient and troubled land of Lemuria, long-buried beneath the ocean waves, Atlan had been conceived, designed, and created as a committed stronghold and repository for the highest levels of the achievements of that long-gone society.

During the 2,265th century following the creation of the nation called Atlan by that small group of Lemurians who were seeking a new start in the world, the second great Golden Age of Atlan began. It was an age of the humanities, of arts and crafts, of music, and growth of the human mind and spirit beyond anything thought possible today.

It was 8000 years later, during the heart of the second Golden Age, that Davol was born.

Although Chedrick's mind was full of questions, he recognized this was a time for listening, not talking. Chedrick's reading, and Davol's chores around the camp, continued late into the day.

When he was satisfied that Chedrick understood the nuances of Traveling and the background of Atlan in Davol's time, the journey began.

Episode 2—Davol at Home

"For this first journey, boy, I will transport us both. Stand near to me, and grasp my hand. Tune into my thoughts and you will see how I do this. Set your mind to be connected to me, and at the same time, hold the intent and desire to see the Atlan of my time."

Once Davol was certain that the boy had followed his instructions, the journey was nearly instantaneous, and both found themselves observing the Atlan that Davol knew as "home."

Chedrick found himself thinking, "I've seen this place before! I've had visions and dreams of this place." The land was green and beautiful. Tasteful stone buildings glistened in the sun. Chedrick could see his own body and that of Davol, as though they were physically standing there. The sun shone brightly, and Chedrick could feel the warmth from it, and was quite comfortable.

He could hear the sounds of children playing in the background and observed as people strode by on the cobblestone path. He could plainly hear their conversation, and even though one gentleman passed within two feet of Chedrick's location, the man showed no hint that he recognized that another person was present.

Davol laughed as he watched Chedrick's head swivel this way and that, trying to take in everything at once.

"It's beautiful, Davol! This is one of the most beautiful places I've ever seen!"

"Look! There's a city over there! And look at those gardens! I wonder where this path leads? What are those people doing over there? I love all the bright colors!" Chedrick's wonder overflowed from his mouth.

A moment later, a small group of people walked by, conversing amongst themselves. "What is this strange language they are speaking?" he asked Davol.

"Listen with your mind, boy, and not your ears."

Chedrick made the mental shift to using telepathic communication instead of hearing. The group was excitedly talking about today's lecturer at Teacher's Park. He understood them perfectly. They were talking excitedly about a guest lecturer called Glarglebarth.

"Oh! Can we go see what they're talking about?" Chedrick asked excitedly.

Davol chuckled. "Of course we can, my boy. That's why I've brought you here. Glarglebarth is an old friend of mine."

Even though, when one is a Traveler, it is unnecessary to physically walk from place to place, our minds create the illusion of walking unless we specifically override it for instantaneous transport. Davol and Chedrick stepped to the well-worn cobblestone path, turned their backs to the city, and followed the group that had just passed.

"We are entering into a reserve which is known as 'Teacher's Park.' It has been used by teachers and students for nearly 20,000 years."

As they followed the path out of the city, they came to a low rise that offered a spectacular view of Atlan's capital city, also known as Atlan, and the surrounding seascape and countryside. Beyond the city, which was spectacular in its own right, the land and grounds were stunningly beautiful. They were vibrant with healthy plants, green and immaculate, and occasional small trees with round tops and slender trunks. There were also occasional small groups of deer wandering through it all, browsing on the foliage without a care.

Davol got Chedrick's attention and then directed that attention to the left and slightly behind them. There was a beautiful half-moon bay to the left, and on the point of land that extended furthest out into the bay, there was a low, square, white building with a shimmering dome of energy that occupied most of its roof.

"That," said Davol, "is one of our power stations. Our

power stations supply the energy that supports the Atlantean way of life. There is a grid of stations around the world, all tied together, and, deep beneath this island, is the master power center, containing a crystal of tremendous size that was placed there by our Star Brothers over 300,000 years ago. All of the other power centers are connected to, and depend on that one."

Then, gesturing directly to the left, to the glistening half-moon bay, Davol continued. "And that is Glarglebarth's home."

Chedrick was simply too overcome with all the newness to question anything that Davol said, and they continued walking along the path.

A few paces past the top of the rise, a lesser path broke off and led forward and to the left. Chedrick could see that it led downhill, and toward the coast. He looked at Davol with questioning eyes, but Davol nodded in the direction of the main path.

A couple of hundred paces later, they came to the top of a second soft rise, a little higher than the first. Another, smaller trail led down the grassy embankment to the right. Chedrick could see, in the mid-distance, a natural granite amphitheater with a series of nine tall stones and several smaller ones, forming a stately backdrop, and an audience of about 35 people seated on the grass facing it.

A tall man in a light blue robe with a short, conical blue hat was addressing the group. Off in the distance, to the left, and over the sea, a small gray shape could be seen in the sky. Although it started out as a mere dot, it grew steadily as Chedrick watched.

The man in blue was speaking. "…and so, as I promised you last week, my good friend Glarglebarth will be our guest lecturer today. He's been doing some fascinating research on the off-planet history of the Selkie folk. As you are all aware, the Selkie have always been very reluctant to talk about their home planet."

By now, the gray spot in the sky resolved itself into a dolphin, and that dolphin gently lowered itself until it hovered, vertically, just above the ground next to the man in blue.

Glarglebarth proceeded to speak for about half an hour. His lecture was full of facts, but also full of mirth, for Glarglebarth really valued a good laugh. He was actually a bit of a jester and could be highly irreverent at times, but he was an excellent teacher.

As Glarglebarth began his presentation, Chedrick, turned to Davol. His lower jaw was actually hanging slack with surprise again.

"How does he do that, Davol? How does he fly like that? How does he float like that?"

"The Dolphinic community that lives in our bay is unique in all the world. The Star Brothers came to them long before humans arrived on this island. The Star Brothers greatly increased their telepathic ability and gave them the ability to levitate. Their delicate skin does not allow them to be in the sun for long, so a guest lecture such as this is a rare and special occasion."

By then, Glarglebarth had completed his talk, and was a rapidly disappearing gray speck in the sky, headed back toward the half-moon bay.

The crowd was dispersing, with little clumps of threes and fours starting to make their way back up the incline where Davol and Chedrick were observing. A few others remained to speak with their teacher.

Chedrick was once more, completely engrossed in the beauty that he saw around him, and was shocked when one of the students actually walked through him on their way back to the city.

"I feel like I'm so real, yet that man just walked through me. He didn't even notice it, and I barely felt it! What a strange thing this Traveling is!"

"That's because your spirit and your consciousness are present here but your body is not," Davol patiently explained. "For all intents and purposes, you are present here, but only for you, and in this case for me as well."

As they talked, Davol followed the crowd back toward the city.

As they entered the main part of the city, Chedrick, once more, could not help but notice the beauty all around them. Even the city was more like living in a pristine, verdant park. The buildings were made of glistening stone, with large open areas around them, and cobblestone paths, worn smooth by many centuries of foot traffic, threaded throughout the city.

Here and there were small knots of people. Some were talking, others were offering the fruits of their labors to any who wanted them, without charge. As a matter of fact, money was unknown to Atlanteans. People did what they loved because they loved it, and took as much or more joy in sharing their creations, as they had in creating them. The Atlantean society was wealthy enough and secure enough that no one ever wanted for anything. It was a society with an economy based on gifting, not selling, or even barter.

Chedrick notices that even though the people around him are conversing, and that he can hear the conversations, nobody's lips are moving. Davol reminds him that Atlanteans were predominantly a telepathic race, and that physical speech was the exception rather than the norm.

"There are three basic levels of telepathy," Davol began. "The first level is 'resting' telepathy or 'passive' telepathy. It is akin to being in a room with a few other people who occasionally, quietly, converse. While you could choose to listen in on their conversation, practicality and courtesy dictate that you would normally just tune it out. If someone were to direct a thought at you, however, you would be instantly attentive and receptive to their communication.

The second level of telepathy is called 'active' or 'communicative' telepathy. This occurs when you 'tune in' to another to in order to check on their health, well-being, mental condition, or concerns, or just to have a conversation. It is the equivalent of saying 'how are you today?' It is also the level of telepathy used for day-to-day conversations.

The third level is not possessed by all, nor is it often required or used. It is called 'broadcast' telepathy. This is the ability to address a large number of people over an extended distance with your thoughts. It is often well developed in many statesmen, teachers, and entertainers.

By being completely open with our thoughts, Atlanteans hold no secrets from one another. In such circumstances, duplicity and criminality are impossible, and any antisocial tendencies are easily detected and dealt with from a very early age, with love, compassion, and corrective redirection. While it is possible to keep secrets, the very act of keeping a secret is very easily detected by those around you and is cause for suspicion.

When you are in complete communication with all of society, mindfulness becomes second nature. If your brother is hurt or in distress, you help him. When you help your sister, you are helping yourself. Of course, as a rule of thumb, having the ability to 'see' carries with it the responsibility never to 'peek.' Our telepathic gift was never to be used to pry into the unnecessary details of another's life, but only to support and assist others."

***

Here and there were small depressions in the carefully groomed lawns. Lined with stone surfaces arranged for seating, they were called "adnesur," meaning "little theater." Each was perhaps 20 paces by 35 paces, shaped like the bowl of a spoon, with four rows of seating rimming the shallow end, and a grassy circle 15 paces in diameter at the low point of the spoon, about half an average person's height in depth. It was there that the speakers or performers would stand.

Davol drifted toward one adnesur where a sizable crowd had gathered. The seating had all been taken and there was a group of people ringing the perimeter, in places, two deep.

As Travelers, Davol and Chedrick had no problem shifting their presence and point-of-view to one that looked over the tops of the other spectator's heads, giving them an unrestricted view of the performance stage.

They did not have to wait very long, as a lithe young woman made her way through the crowd and stepped into the center stage.

With a practiced shimmy, the young woman stepped free of her krut and out of her tuks, those ornate, flat sandals currently in fashion, and down, into the sunken, circular heart of the small adnesur. Her teen-aged daughter and young son sat at the lip at the back of the adnesur, with their mother between them and the majority of the audience. She began swaying, moving her limbs to some seductive, unheard music, moving like a tall reed in a brisk wind. Chedrick's mind was immediately filled with soul-touching, ethereal music, and a display of colors beyond anything he had ever seen or imagined completely filled his perception. The music and colors coordinated and contrasted with one another in an exquisite, all-encompassing "dance of the senses."

Chedrick was astonished to find tears, or the perception of tears, flowing from his eyes. The joy of the experience was beyond anything he had ever known. He looked at other members of the audience and discovered that many of them also had blissful looks on their faces, large smiles, and tears flowing down their cheeks as well.

Chedrick had no explanation for what was happening. He turned to his mentor with questions in his eyes only to find that the old Wizard was also weeping.

"What is this, Davol? What's happening? What is she doing?"

Davol, lost in reverie, shook himself free, wiped his eyes, and answered.

"Yes, she is remarkable, isn't she? She is one of the best energy artists of my long lifetime. She paints with sounds and colors in the minds of her audience, and she is one of the top energy artisans in all of Atlan. She is able to create colors, pictures, and music in the minds of her audience. Each one hears and sees their own unique presentation, yet all have similar experiences. There are very few energy artists. It is truly a gift.

Her name is Toibl."

Toibl's 5-year-old son slyly pushed one of his mother's tuks off the lip of the adnesur and grinned impishly as it came to rest near his mother's dancing feet. His sister turned toward him and silently admonished him. Still grinning impishly, he sat back on his perch.

Chedrick turned back to Davol, a little surprised to see the old man still wiping tears from his eyes and a hint of deep sadness in his eyes.

"Tell me about your life here, Davol," Chedrick asked.

Davol turned, and stepped away from the crowd, following one of the paths back toward Teacher's Park.

After a few moments, the old man gathered his composure and began telling Chedrick of his life in old Atlan.

"I am the last of the line of House Namor, a house of noble star blood mixed with human. When I was 12 years old, the Star Brothers took me to their home planet, where I was educated for 35 years.

I remember well the day that I returned from the stars to Atlan. I was still very young, only 47 years old, with a long life ahead of me. Freshly graduated from my basic education pattern on the Star Brother's planets. I stood at Pujar-lin-Marakep the extinct volcano that is the highest point on the central island of Atlan and surveyed my home planet, Earth. I looked toward the Northwest, over the short distance of calm ocean waters to the inner ring of lands and islands that surrounded us. In the distance, I could see the outer ring, home to the seafarers, the farmers, and the crafts people's communities. The central island was reserved for, and nourished, the arts, advanced learning, and culture of our nation. Turning around, I saw below me our beautiful, glistening capital city, which we also call Atlan.

Atlan, our nation, was created a little over 3000 centuries ago, in large part by the ancient technology of the Star people. I marveled at the perfect slices of granite and marble of our magnificent Atlantean city, and how they sparkled in the morning sun. To the right, I saw the point of land that housed one of Atlan's major power stations. The one I showed you earlier.

Because of my blood heritage, and my off-world education, I was offered immediate entrance as a member of the Grand Council. I was also appointed as a teacher and held classes nearly every day in Teacher's Park.

More than forty years passed, and one day, one of my colleagues brought his infant daughter, Toibel, to the teachers' relaxation area in order to show her off.

Because Atlanteans have such a long life expectancy, normally one hundred and eighty to two hundred years, and because of our lifelong training in mindfulness, most followed the unofficial guideline of one child per person in order to avoid overpopulation, so having a child was a very large event in someone's life.

Meamo, my colleague, proudly presented his daughter to his colleagues that morning. My friends and I all had to laugh because when she cried, her eyes would scrunch up, she would purse her lips together, her face would turn red, and her cheeks would puff out. Somebody commented that she reminded him of the little puffer fish that was common in our seas.

The Atlantean name for that little puffer fish was Toibl, so we began calling her Toibl, and that became her nickname."

"Her father left a few years later, to teach in one of our colonies.

I did not see her again for almost forty years, and when she returned to Atlan, she brought with her, her 8-year-old daughter. It was quite unusual to have a child at such an early age, but Toibl was an artist, and a bit rebellious. She had lived with another artist, a young man who was native to the land where her father was teaching, and the child, Eetat, had been born to her when she was only 30 years old.

Because her father had been part of the teaching community, Toibl found a second home among the teachers and students of Atlan.

Over the span of a couple of years, Toibl and I discovered deep compatibility with one another, and decided that we would live together.

Because of my status as a senior instructor and a member of the Grand Council, I was allowed to live in a very beautiful area on the outskirts of the city, on a forested hillside overlooking the sea.

Shortly after moving in together, Toibl became pregnant, and soon, I had my one and only child, a boy named Robognom. We called him Robo, and he brought me more joy than I have ever known. He was the sun in my sky, and the moon and stars in my night.

Robo adored his big sister Tattie and followed her everywhere, as soon as he was able.

By the time she was sixteen, Tattie was intensely interested in herbs and herbal healing and would go on long forages in the woods above where we lived, taking Robo in tow.

One afternoon in early summer, as Toibl and I were sunning ourselves in the meadow, and Tattie was working with her herbs, Robo decided to explore our little paradise on his own. He was 5 years old.

On the seaward side of our homestead, where the grassy meadow slopes up into the ancient forest, there is a beautiful view of the sea from the top of a 30-foot cliff. It was one of my favorite spots, and I spent many hours standing there, alone, deep in thought, and gazing at the sea.

Robo must've been enjoying that view when the cliff edge crumbled under his foot, sending him tumbling down the 30-foot embankment and breaking his neck."

By now, the old man's tears were flowing openly, and his voice was choked with emotion. He covered his face with his hands and struggled valiantly to continue his story.

The Wizard's voice filtered jaggedly through his hands. "Tattie found her brother later that day.

Shortly after that, Tattie left to go live with her father. Toibl stayed with me for another 70 years, before she, too, left to explore the world."

Chedrick interrupted. "… And that dancer we saw, the energy artist. You said her name was Toibl? And the little boy, and the girl?"

Copious tears flowed, unabashed, down the old man's cheeks.

"Pardon me for a few moments, boy," the old Wizard said as he disappeared from Chedrick's awareness.

About half an hour later, Davol returned.
No words were necessary.
Or possible.

Episode 3—Other Worlds, Other Lives

Some time later, in the deep forest they called 'home', Davol seemed to have fully recovered his normal composure and emotional balance after the Atlantean journey.

"Would you like to know a little more background about the Atlan of my time, boy?" the Wizard asked one day while the two were having their mid-day meal.

Without waiting for Chedrick to swallow and reply, he continued.

"From about the age of two years, until they were about 12 years old, our children gather together in outdoor classrooms where they were taught the basics of Atlantean education. The lessons included mindfulness of others; consideration of others over self, how to know and appreciate their innate energetic gifts, and an opportunity to find those interests that appealed most strongly to them. We encouraged them to know and appreciate their connectedness to one another, the planet, and life itself.

Mindfulness occurs when one remains constantly aware and attuned to the wants, needs, and desires of others. When one takes action to support or improve another's condition, that is called Love. So, Mindfulness is the component of Love that prompts action."

Chedrick sat, listening and chewing. He knew this was no time to interrupt.

"As our children approached 12 years of age, and when it was deemed by their elders that they had achieved the goals of their early education, it became time for the children to begin to move out into the world as young adults. Many continued to live with their parents, while others had other plans.

By the time most individuals had reached the age of 18 to 20 years, they were considered mature enough and focused enough to enter into what we would call 'employment' today. That is to say, they would find an area of strong interest to them and a way to employ that interest that benefited society. They would then find or create an opportunity to do so. Because of the extremely long life span of the average Atlantean, it was not uncommon for an individual to remain in a state of relatively constant 'employment' for over 100 years. When an individual does what they love, there is no reason to stop doing it, is there, boy?

Thanks to the technology of our Star Brothers, our society was largely self-sustaining without any need of a labor force, so many went into the arts. Others went into areas that supported society as a whole in more material ways. It was always a matter of free choice, as were the hours and days, or years, worked. Because the citizens were allowed to follow their muse, what we would call "employment" was actually a very pleasurable activity."

"So everyone does a task they love, that they choose?" Chedrick asked.

"Exactly, my boy. Thanks to the gifts of technology from our Star Brothers, people were free to choose anything they wished; art, music, leadership, gardening, cleaning and maintenance, research, languages, education, or cooking.

Thus, it was, at a very high level, that in Atlantean society, each gave as they could and took as they needed, while always mindful of the needs of others. It was also very much a meritocracy, and those who excelled in their field and dedicated themselves to their chosen task were rewarded accordingly.

Just a couple more things, boy, and I'll shut up for a while and let you finish your meal," the old Wizard said.

"The governing body of Atlan consisted of a 'Grand Council,' which, in turn, consisted of a 'High Council' of those who had proved meritorious in their various endeavors, and a 'Council Emeritus' consisting of High Council members who had served with merit for more than 75 years. There was also a 'Star Council.' These were the most experienced and most highly regarded of the 'Grand Council' chosen especially for their ability to make wise decisions and to work closely with our many Star Brothers. Approximately ten percent of the Grand Council, by number and by merit, comprised the Presidium. The Presidium oversaw the day-to-day governmental functions of Atlan.

Now, eat, boy."

Episode 4—Gareth Zed and Atlan's First Golden Age

Chedrick was uncharacteristically silent for the next few hours, following the meal. Finally, sitting with his back toward his mentor, he spoke. "Traveling with you, and seeing your home, your people, your family, has shown me how very small the world of my experience has been."

Turning toward the Wizard, Chedrick made eye contact and continued. "It has also made me very curious as to what else is out there that I have not yet seen."

"You had told me that you lived during the second Golden Age of Atlan, but you have never told me anything about the first Golden Age. What was that like, Davol?"

It was Davol's turn to be silent for a while.

"An excellent question, boy. Our first Golden Age occurred in a world that was far different from the one you observed. It endured for nearly 200,000 years and was a glorious time. Our Star Brothers had taken us under their wing, educating, nurturing, and guiding Atlan on an active, daily basis. They had a far greater presence than what you saw. It was impossible to take even a short walk without seeing several of our Star Brothers.

Then, about 20,000 years ago, for their own reasons, almost all of them left Earth. There followed 2000 years of adjustment and rebalancing for the Atlanteans. Our Star Brothers had left behind their wonderful technologies, and the knowledge of how to use those technologies to maintain our high standard of living, but the psychological shock of having lost those whom we had learned to depend on for guidance took quite a long while to overcome. Perhaps that is the very reason they chose to leave.

But, back to your question, boy. We can indeed Travel to

a time during the first Golden Age that you may find very interesting. That is, if you'd like to do that?" Davol said with a huge grin and a mischievous twinkle in his eye.

Chedrick's eyes lit up like a pair of full moons. "Yes! Of course! When do we leave?"

"We shall leave in the morning, after a good night's rest. In the meantime, I'll tell you a little bit about what we'll see and experience.

When the continent of Lemuria sank beneath the waves in the far distant past, small bands of Lemurians explored the world for a sheltered land, free of strife, and of temperate climate, in which to rebuild their society. One such group came upon our beautiful island nation of Atlan.

Our Star Brothers, whom we had known from Lemuria, had returned to Earth after a prolonged absence, and, when our people arrived and discovered this land, helped us build our nation. For their own reasons, the Star Brothers had decided that Atlan was an ideal location for their regional headquarters in our star system. In addition to using their incredibly advanced technology to help us build a capital city, literally overnight, they linked parts of some of their cities on their home planets to Atlan's location on Earth.

The resulting city, was, for many centuries, one of the most spectacular sites imaginable. The shining white stone of the simple but elegant Atlantean buildings was impressive by itself. But above that… Ah! Above that floated crystal cathedrals; buildings made of pure energy, reaching to the sky itself. Buildings that did not exist on earth, but were visible to earthlings, and accessed through levitation devices by those on the ground. These exquisite structures were direct links to the Star Brother's home worlds. Our Star Brothers also used a variety of small, silvery individual craft to move between the floating buildings, and there was a steady stream of these vehicles moving silently but purposefully through the air above our capital.

There was perhaps a score of planets represented, each with its own distinctive life form. Some looked just like you and I. Some looked like us, but were twice as tall. Some reminded me of man-birds with blue feathers. Some were tall, with shiny golden skin and huge dark eyes; but all had come here to help us.

Under the care of our Star Brothers, extremely long lifetimes were not unusual."

"You mean like yours, Davol?" Chedrick asked.

Davol chuckled. "No, boy. I mean LOOONG lifetimes. The man I am proposing to visit is, at the time we will see him, just over 11,000 years old."

"Is he a Star Brother then?" Chedrick asked.

"Not precisely, my boy. Like most Atlanteans of his time, his bloodline was deeply colored with Star Brother traits, including longevity. The man we are going to visit is called 'Gareth Zed,' and his full title was 'Defender of the Emerald Tablets of the Laws, and Confidant of Thoth, the Atlantean.'

Let me tell you a little more about the history of Atlan, boy. One of the things that first drew the small band of Lemurians to the land that would become Atlan was a barely visible, brightly shimmering speck in the sky above the sea when viewed from the mainland. Determined to find out what this was, the group set out in their ships and sailed toward the setting sun. After sailing for 3 days, they found themselves in a small, half-moon bay. It was located on a large central island with concentric rings of islands surrounding it, buffering it from the sea. Floating above them, twice as high as a man could shoot an arrow, was a floating city in the sky. The buildings were so tall they reached up almost to the very heavens, and from time to time, one could see sparks and glimmers, shimmering energy outlining each building against the sky. Now blue, now purple, then back to blue. Hints and sparkles of color, rather than solid sheets. From time to time, they could see round platforms floating in midair, going slowly between the buildings. Occasionally they would see the small craft, shaped much like an apple seed, made of silver, moving more quickly through the air."

"The city cast no shadow upon the sea.

The dwellers of the city seemed to pay no attention to the ships below. Nothing threatened the sailors, or vessels. The

Lemurians spoke among themselves. Some recalled legends from the old land of the Star Brothers and their miraculous cities.

A landing party was sent ashore, and the land was found to be ideal for colonization. The ground was rich and unspoiled, there were many freshwater springs, and, with the exception of one large mountain, the land was gently sloped and welcoming.

And thus, Atlan was born.

The Atlanteans settled the rich land and, after fending for themselves for nearly 500 years, the Star Brothers initiated contact and began sharing their science, technology, knowledge, and gifts with the Atlantean people. Eventually, a few Atlanteans were invited to visit the crystal city, floating above the bay.

Little by little, with the passage of time, the two cultures became more deeply intertwined, and while very few Atlanteans were invited to the city in the clouds, it was extremely common to see and interact with Star Brothers in the city of Atlan. Occasionally, romance blossomed between the two groups, resulting in gifted and exceptionally long-lived offspring."

Episode 5—Gareth

"Gareth Zed was one of these. During the time of Gareth Zed, the Star Brothers, a term that encompasses many different races from many different star systems, constituted nearly half of Atlan's population. Earth, and Atlan, were, at that time, major outposts and centers for this sector of the Milky Way galaxy.

The technology of the Star Brothers was so advanced that buildings were not built, they were simply manifested, and they manifested without a lot of regard for gravity. The structures were composed of matter deposited directly from the ethers. They did not require heating, cooling, or air conditioning and could be made translucent or transparent at will, resulting in tall, stately skyscrapers, seemingly made of crystal, with unlikely and gravity-defying proportions and design.

Gareth had been specially selected by Thoth when he was a youth of only 470 years and had undergone extensive education processes on many planets over several centuries. At the point in his life where we shall meet him, at the pinnacle of his career, Gareth Zed was the closest human assistant to one of the highest and most revered of all the Star Brothers of all time.

Gareth was a very wise and gifted man, powerful, yet of great compassion. He had served as Thoth's top human liaison for nearly 10,000 years.

Thoth, the Atlantean, was an extremely high level, full-blood Star Brother. He was a Prince of an esteemed imperial line on his home planet. He was one of the most intelligent beings ever known, one of the three leaders of the Star Brothers on Earth, and a true master of energetics in every sense. Some saw him as a god."

Chedrick took his eyes off of his mentor's face for a moment and happened to look down. If he had been truly wearing his body he would've jumped as high as the tallest trees back home!

"Davol! We're flying!"

Davol gave the boy a look. "No, boy, we're not flying at all. Even though you see me and I see you, we are not here in the physical. If we had brought our bodies along for this trip, we would be flying. We are only here as pure consciousness, and pure consciousness exists everywhere. We are only shifting our awareness of what position we are viewing things from. I'm taking you to view Gareth Zed."

Floating through space and walls and force fields with equal ease, Davol brought Chedrick's consciousness into a room in the tallest tower of the city. There was a man standing at a large window with his back to them. The man appeared to be quite tall, human, with a robust build that somehow was impressive without being intimidating. He stood, obviously deep in thought, with his hands locked behind his back, and rocked back and forth slightly on his feet as his thoughts ran their course.

"This is Gareth Zed, boy. He has been working on one of Thoth's greatest projects, and they are in the final phases of beginning to implement it."

Gareth, still standing with his back to them, clasped and unclasped his hands, and nodded his head several times, as though he had come to an agreement with himself.

He turned slowly, eyes scanning the room. "Who are you? I know you're here. I can feel you." His form was firm without being plump, his face weathered and time-aged, and was just beginning to show noticeable wrinkles. His white hair was close cut to his skull. All in all, a man best described as a ruggedly handsome older man with kind eyes.

Chedrick turned questioning eyes toward the old Wizard. "Are you going to tell him we are here? Are you going to tell him who we are?"

It is barely possible that Davol might have rolled his eyes just a little bit. "Do you not remember me telling you that those whom we observe when Traveling cannot see us or hear us? Gareth is a truly great adept; one of the finest the world has ever seen, so he knew we were here the moment we arrived."

"Come here boy," Davol said as he drifted toward the large window. "I want you to see something."

Chedrick's intent to do so transported him instantly to Davol's side, facing the window.

"Where is your island, Davol? Where's Atlan?"

Chedrick's alarm was obvious.

"Follow me, boy," Davol repeated, as he drifted through the window to the outside of the building. "Now look down," the Wizard commanded.

Chedrick complied and again was obviously astonished. "There it is! It wasn't there a minute ago."

"Now go back inside and look out through the window again."

Again, Chedrick complied, but only for a moment. He rushed back to Davol's side outside the building. He looked down, then looked at the old wizard, puzzled.

"When I'm inside the building, there's no Atlan. When I'm outside the building, Atlan is right there!" He looked once more at his teacher with questioning eyes.

"This building that Gareth resides in, and all the other buildings of this city, do not exist on Earth. The building floats above the endless seas of the Council planet of T'Chlin. Over a million years ago, the Star Council choose the planet of T'Chlin as a neutral ground in perpetuity, a safe place for all races to come together for the benefit of all races. T'Chlin was a planet with no land, only sea. That is why, when you are inside the building, you see only sea, but when you are outside the building, in Earth's atmosphere, you see Atlan. While there was abundant life in T'Chlin's seas, that life had never evolved to the point of civilization or science. Because of this, it had been declared a neutral location by the Star Council. Floating cities were established in its skies, the smaller ones acting as embassies for their home planets. The largest city, Estreo, home of the Star Brothers' judicial and regulatory activities, and meeting place for the Star Council, is the city that we see from Atlan. It is an energetic reflection of Estero, complete in every way, manifesting in the skies of Earth. It is also a direct connection through space and time to the original. When we enter this building, we are on T'Chlin. When we exit it, we are on Earth."

Chedrick discovered that his mouth was agape once more, and closed it. "Can we visit some of the other worlds, then?"

"Certainly, but perhaps not on this visit."

Davol continued "There were 923 races and cultures represented on the Star Council and thirteen on the Grand Council. Thoth was one of those thirteen, the most senior member, and the most respected. At the time, he was 460,000 Earth-years old, and wise beyond words."

"…and what was Thoth's grand plan that Gareth was working on Davol?"

"You may have heard of a land called Egypt. In your time, it was a great sand desert, barely habitable. Two hundred thousand years ago, it was a lush and fertile land. In it, there lived another group of Lemurian refugees; a group that had forgotten their past, and had reverted to a very primitive way of life.

It was Thoth's plan to begin to reintroduce to the Egyptian's their knowledge, arts, and science. Much had been lost in their long journey from Lemuria, including their knowledge of the Star Brothers. Thoth and Gareth had formulated a long-term plan to restore what had been lost to time."

Episode 6—The Plan

"Since the Egyptians were prone to believing in Gods, Thoth, and several of the other Star Brothers, along with a large group of Atlanteans would sail in a magnificent ship into the mouth of the Nile River to make a grand entrance at Egypt's largest city. There would be a great display of finery and wealth, and the Star Brothers would assume the appearance of oversized humans with animal heads in order to command the attention of the Egyptian citizens.

The plan was for the Star Brothers to come-and-go over several thousand years, and for the Atlantean cadre to reside there in Egypt permanently, as the spokesmen and liaisons between the Egyptians and their new gods, the Star Brothers. The Atlanteans would oversee the education of the Egyptian people, bringing back the arts, science, and music their society had lost in the long years of migration. Due to his position with Thoth, Gareth also would come-and-go, acting as an overseer to the entire program for nearly 5000 years."

"Wow," Chedrick said. "I wish I could be around to see all that!"

"Well, my boy, one of the nice things about Traveling is that, just like you can pop in and out of this building at will, you can pop in and out of any point in time, at any location you like. You can see 5000 years of progress in an hour if you choose. Today is not the day, but if you like, we can travel together another time to observe as civilization comes to primitive Egypt. Would you like that?"

"Yes, sir. I'd like that very much."

"Today's journey was to show you more of Atlan's history, and to introduce you to Gareth Zed and Thoth the Atlantean."

"We're going to meet Thoth, then?" Chedrick asked excitedly.

Davol chuckled. "One does not meet Thoth. One experiences Thoth. It took Gareth Zed many years of training to be capable of communicating effectively with Thoth. Those who call Thoth a God are not far from wrong. His perceptions, thoughts, and abilities are simply so far beyond mere humans that communication as we know it is simply not adequate. Only the most highly trained human adepts can begin to communicate with him, or understand him.

Thoth, Gareth Zed, and their team will bring civilization to Egypt, and from Egypt, they will touch their world with much that has been lost.

There are lands that you have never heard of, boy, that the Egyptian mages, trained and guided by Atlanteans, will colonize. Many years in the future, there will be portals built, deep underground, below massive monuments that will last for thousands of years. There will be a great Library under the ground, containing all the knowledge of the world.

Those who are trained by and have the abilities of the Atlanteans will be able to stand within these portals, facing a certain direction, holding their hands and body in a certain pose, and, by thinking certain thoughts, instantly transport themselves and their bodies to lands and places beyond your dreams. They will travel to a lake in a land you've never heard of, halfway around the world, through a portal known as the Island of the Sun to the local indigenous people. They will travel to the highest mountains of the world, to secret cities hidden high in those mountain valleys, to share our secret knowledge with the holy people living there. All these things they will do, taking their physical bodies, clothes, tools, and implements with them, through the power of their minds, and the secrets of the Atlanteans. That is Thoth's grand plan."

"I want to see all of that! How can I see all of it?"

Davol's friendly chuckle filled the air. "You're so impatient, lad. You have a long life ahead of you. I think that, for today, we are done. There are other lifetimes and other wonders that I would like to show you. Let us return back home to our forest."

Episode 7—Minus Two. Plus One

Just as the first shafts of sunlight touched his eyelids. Chedrick became aware of the excited chittering of Faeries. Rubbing the sleep from his eyes, he rolled out of bed and saw that Davol was conversing with three of them, flitting in front of his face and jabbering excitedly among themselves. Davol motioned him over. "You need to hear this, boy!

The Faerie have brought good news! Acorn's pupa has hatched! He's officially a dad! He has a daughter, and they've named her Flit! We've been invited to come to visit and join in the welcoming celebration in ten days' time!"

"We're going to go, aren't we? That Faerie wedding was beautiful!"

Davol laughed. "Of course we're going boy. The Faerie folk are well known for their celebrations."

Chedrick thought for a moment, then spoke. "Speaking of traveling, Davol, when can we go back to the time of Gareth Zed and Thoth to see more about their plan for Egypt?"

"A fair question, boy. To an accomplished Traveler, time really has no meaning, just as distance really has no meaning. I am in the process of teaching you how to do it for yourself. There will come a time when you will decide to go and just DO it. I may not always be with you, but I will always be easy to find."

Before Chedrick could ask any questions, Davol continued. "In the meantime, boy, are you ready for another Traveling journey? This will be a short one. Several hundred years into your world's future."

Chedrick took the hint, bit back the many questions Davol's statement had awakened, and said, "I'd love to! Where are we going this time?"

"We will be going forward several centuries, here in England, to a time when many nations are at war. You will find that world to be very strange to you also, with carriages that travel the roads without horses. We will arrive in the evening, and it might seem to you that the city is abandoned. There will be no lights to be seen, and barely anyone on the streets."

"Why is that, Davol?"

"Remember the silver ships we saw in the air during our visit to Gareth Zed? Mankind has rediscovered how to make machines that fly through the air. Because Man has forgotten that we all depend on one another, these machines are used to drop fire and death on the innocent people below them. In order not to be found, the people hide indoors, darkening their windows so no trace of light can be seen by the men in the flying ships. There are other flying ships, full of fire and death, that have no men in them. They fly over the ocean, and when they run out of fuel, they drop where they will, destroying factories, homes, farms, and lives.

We shall pay a brief visit to a young lady named Sarah Bottomsly, whom just that day had celebrated her 12th birthday, quietly, indoors, with her parents, three friends, and her little brother, Edwin. Are you ready then, boy?"

Chedrick nodded assent, and in a moment, they were off to the future London Davol had described. It was wintertime, the streets were wet, and traces of snow could be seen here and there. Evening had come to the city, and, without lights, the streets appeared dark and dreary. Only one lone policeman could be seen, silently walking his lonely beat.

They drifted along the street for a way, Chedrick's head on a swivel as he took in the vast newness around him. Finally, Davol stopped, and said, "Well, this is it, boy. This is our destination."

Chedrick looked up at the three-story brick building before him. It looked almost identical to every other building on the block.

"Follow me, boy. It's the flat on the 2nd floor, on the left."

In a trice, the two Travelers were in the flat. Davol led

the way to the children's bedroom. Edwin was fast asleep, but Sarah, filled with the excitement of her birthday and her new doll, was playing quietly at her bedside, with only a single short candle in a pewter candle holder, for light. Her candle's flame sputtered occasionally but provided adequate illumination. She is playing with the doll that her parents had gotten her for her birthday, even though it was well past her bedtime, and she was supposed to be asleep.

"I think I shall call you Betsy," Sarah told her curly-haired doll, as she snuggled her and touched her painted cheek. "We shall have such gay times together!"

Outside, the world was silent and dark. Off in the distance, barely discernible, was a rapid buzzing sound that gradually got louder and louder.

Sarah slowly became aware of the sputtering sound outside, like an automobile repeatedly backfiring. It seemed to be coming closer and closer! But then, it fell silent. She had heard that noise before, just before the loud explosions that had shaken her home. After that came the sounds of the fire brigades rushing to put out flames, rescue the injured, and recover the dead. Hermione, her best friend, told her that the building next door to her had been hit, and told her all about the screams of fear and pain, the rushing rescuers, and the chaotic, fire-lit scene.

For the shortest instant, Sarah felt as though she has been struck by a wall, then, everything quickly faded to darkness, and Sarah and Edwin ceased to be, along with their flat.

As the building collapsed through a stunned Chedrick, leaving him floating in the dust-filled air that, a moment before, had been a London flat. Bricks and debris flew through the space he would've occupied had he been wearing his body. He turned to Davol in shock and dismay.

"What happened, Davol. What happened to Sarah? What happened to the building? What was that explosion? Why did you bring me here to see this?" Chedrick asked, with tears in his eyes.

"I brought you here to help teach you that all life is precious. Sarah, her family, her building and many others were just destroyed by one of the mindless flying machines that simply ran out of fuel and crashed randomly."

"That's terrible. Davol! She was just 12 years old! She was just getting started in life and her brother Edwin! Just a baby!" Chedrick trailed off into speechlessness.

"I brought you here, boy, to make a point about life by observing death. We've spent hours talking about how we have a body, but our body is not us. There comes a time in life when we are put in a position of either living what we say we believe, or no longer being able to say we believe it.

Yes, young Sarah and her baby brother were killed tonight. Was their essence harmed, boy? Or will they come back again, in a different time and a different place, with different bodies, and other lessons to learn?

Some souls, in their eternal sojourn, find it helpful to revisit the material realm in a physical form for a brief moment, in order to better process events and experiences from a previous life. Once that has been accomplished, there is no real need to maintain a physical body, and they return to the realm of energy until they determine that another full lifetime is appropriate for them."

"So, they come back to earth to be human again?" Chedrick questioned.

"Boy, boy, boy! Have I taught you nothing? Look up at the sky. See all those stars? Do you think for one moment that this planet, this species, is all there is? Many of us do return to our familiar haunts, and to those souls that we have traveled through time with. In order to do that, we do return, mostly as humans, to planet Earth. We could also choose to be reborn as a Star Brother on one of their planets, or, here on earth as a dog, a cat, an Ent, a falcon, or a Faerie. Our universe is without limits, boy, and so are we."

With that, Davol shifted his focus, and the two found themselves once more in their forest home. Chedrick remained unusually silent and thoughtful for the next few days, as he processed all he had seen, heard, and experienced.

***

It was late spring in their forest. The woods were alive with the sound of small creatures going about the business of life. Fledgling birds could be heard in the many nests hidden high in the mossy branches. The numerous gray squirrels threw challenges back and forth through the air and chased one another through the limbs and foliage, as they scrambled for territory and mates. The earth itself was rich with the vibrant green of new life and the smells of spring.

It was on such a day, with the warm sun shining, filtered through the trees, and a light fragrant breeze playing in the air, that both Davol and Chedrick succumbed to the serene warmth. Both fell under the tranquil spell of the day, and fell asleep for a late morning nap.

...until Faeries burst upon the scene, chittering and laughing loudly, their wings flashing iridescent sparkles into the air, tumbling over one another in playful joy.

Davol and Chedrick both awakened instantly.

"Tomorrow! Tomorrow is the day we welcome Flit to our community!" Bark, a large, colorful female in her prime, was the group's spokesperson. "Please tell us you'll be there! We have a special surprise for you!"

Bark was quickly elbowed by another of the Faeries, who shot her a scolding look, as though she had given away a big secret. Apple, the second Faerie, quickly pushed in front of Bark and took over the conversation with Davol.

"We would be oh, so happy if you and Chedrick could attend our clan gathering to celebrate the hatchling, Flit!" she said, with a sidelong glance at Bark, warning her against adding anything.

Chedrick looked at Davol and found approval in those wise blue eyes. He spoke up excitedly. "Yes! We'll be there. We'll be there for sure!"

The following morning, Davol and Chedrick were ready before dawn. Davol had been teaching Chedrick how to take his body with him when Traveling, after cautioning him about the many dangers and risks involved. The trip to the Faery gathering would be Chedrick's first attempt to Travel on his own, while in body.

"Go ahead, lad. I'll be there soon," Davol told the boy, as he fussed unnecessarily with his duffel.

Heart in his throat, Chedrick performed the mental exercises Davol had taught him, set his intention, and…

…materialized at the edge of the clearing where the celebration of Flit's hatch was to be celebrated! Davol manifested there a moment later, nudged Chedrick, and moved toward the celebration.

Now, it must be said that the Faerie folk really know how to throw a party. Being very colorful beings physically, living a relatively carefree life in the deep woods, and excelling in handicrafts and artistic expression over tens of thousands of years, they have perfected the art of celebration!

Everyone was dressed in the finest finery. Every jewel in every garment glistened, and every carapace was hand-rubbed with a natural wax to bring out its natural luster and iridescent colors. The celebrations were always held in Spring, so even the forest was dressed in its brightest colors, blossoms, and finery.

There were more Faerie folk there than Chedrick had ever seen before! There must have been several thousand of the delightful, small beings scattered across the natural meadow on the forest floor.

One of the most beautiful aspects of the gathering was that every partnered adult had worn their nuptial cloaks the epitome of Faerie handiwork and beauty. To observe the gathering was to observe a living kaleidoscope truly breathtaking and unforgettable.

The Matriarch, in her resplendent cloak, walked purposely to the center of the meadow and clicked loudly, three times in rapid succession.

A silence fell over the crowd, and everyone moved silently into the woods around the meadow. Only the old and infirm remained at the periphery, to watch.

The Matriarch raised both her arms and her wings above her head and began singing one of the beautiful Faerie chants welcoming Spring, as the multitude joined in.

A joyful, colorful procession of Faerie folk entered the meadow from all sides in twos and threes, in seven lines from seven directions, filing into the center of the meadow to where the Matriarch stood. When all were assembled, it looked much like a colorful but slightly ragged, seven-pointed star made of Faeries.

Simultaneously, all began singing another bright and cheerful Faerie anthem, welcoming spring, and every newborn of that year.

Faerie singing… There is absolutely nothing like it in the universe. In addition to the high chittering, the clicks. and the profound silences, the males were capable of producing a deep, almost subsonic, thrumming bass counterpoint. Add to this the visual effect of seeing thousands of small, bejeweled, iridescent bodies joyfully moving in time with the intoxicating rhythm, and you have a small clue as to what it is like to witness Faerie singing firsthand.

The next song was more somber and slower-paced. It spoke of those departed, of the losses of the past year, and the disappointments experienced both individually and as a people. At the end of the song, the cadence picked up, and the song brightened noticeably, in recognition of the knowledge that what had seemed like a tragedy yesterday will reveal itself as a boon tomorrow, and those who have laid down their bodies will someday return in new ones.

At the end of that song, the Faerie folk closest to the Matriarch took flight, swirling upward in a tight spiral. As each group took flight, those behind them stepped forward and lifted themselves into the air, joining the ever-growing, living column of sparkling color lifting itself into the sky. When the column reached almost the height of the surrounding trees, the Faeries at the top circled round in a larger circle, creating what looked like a ball of color at the top of the column.

When all but a few hundred of the Fae had become

part of the massive structure, with the remaining Faeries still in their ragged, seven-pointed star around the Matriarch, the entire group, except for the Matriarch, suddenly exploded off in different directions, filling the air with the biggest Burst of Faeries imaginable.

The ceremony was full of meaning. The seven groups entering the meadow represented the ancient seven clans of Fae from G|bo*sh. their home planet. The shape of the flight represented a tree, mother to their race in the far, distant past. Trees gave them safety, security, and lodging as they grew from insectoids to rational beings over millennia. The final, spectacular burst represented fertility. The tree, spreading its seeds, the Fae, traveling to the stars.

While all attention was on the spectacular air display, Acorn and three other fathers rapidly approached the Matriarch from the forest just behind her, with their children trotting excitedly alongside them. The fathers placed their children at the Matriarch's feet, facing the crowd, urged them to behave, and slipped back into the woods.

"Friends, Family, and Fae," the Matriarch boomed.

"Life is a gift, and a new life is the greatest gift. Today we celebrate the hatching of four pupae, four new lives to add to our community.

Let the fathers come forth, and stand by your child."

Acorn and the three other fathers stepped from the woods and stood proudly next to their offspring. The children stood next to their fathers. One cuddled his father's leg for security, and another held her father's hand tightly.

"Each of you has held your larva within your shell, beneath the Cre'upsun, nestled among your three hearts, and under your hardened wings, protected and nourished by your own juices for over two years."

It was easy to tell when a Faerie child was about to be born. The larva that first crawled into the cavity below the father's wing was only an inch long, but over the long gestation period, it grew to almost full-grown Faerie size, complete with wings, arms legs, and the rest of the accouterments of an adult.

Some were as long as 9 inches! This caused the father to slouch further and further forward as the gestation progresses. By the end of the gestation, some fathers were so bent over that it was nearly impossible to walk any distance.

"One of our fathers has elected to choose a P*arsh|-ta'ush for their child. Davol loch Namor, you have been nominated. Do you accept?"

There was a loud click between the "p" and the "a," made by a special part of the Faerie's carapace, and a hole in the word, between the syllables, that sucked all sound out of the air.

All eyes turned toward Davol.

P*arsh|ta'ush is a combination of the Faerie words for Grandfather and wise elder.

Most humans never even try to pronounce Faerie words as the Faerie do, but simply make the sounds that come the closest to pronouncing the words they hear. The Faerie understand. Humans are, comparatively, very limited in their speech capabilities. The first word, P*arsh,| meant respected elder male relative, and the second word, ta'ush, is best translated as "wise teacher." To the Faerie folk, being a P*arsh|ta'ush was equivalent to being a godfather and wise life advisor all rolled into one. It was both quite an honor and quite a responsibility. In the long, long, history of the Fae, this was the first time a human had ever been asked to be the overseer, or P*arsh|ta'ush, as the Faerie said.

Davol stepped forward into the center of the gathering, standing next to Acorn with Flit between them. Taking Flit's hand, he replied, "I do accept, Matriarch."

Acorn reaches into an embroidered pouch at his side and produces an oval-shaped, ridged, and semi-transparent, thin oval plate, which he hands to Davol.

Davol accepts the small, hard, slightly convex shell that covered Flit during her incubation. Faerie children are born able to speak and walk. They learn speech because of what they hear through their father's shell. Telepathy usually develops a couple of years later. A Faerie's first flight usually occurs when they have been hatched for a year.

They all turned to face the Matriarch, who said to Davol, "This Cre'upsun protected her when she was young. Will you watch after her, guide her, and protect her as she grows?"

"I will," said Davol

And with that, it was done.

With the formalities out of the way, the next three days were days of song and dance, of joy and beauty. Faeries put on plays, held cooking contests, and displayed their handiwork and fine embroidery. Many gifts were exchanged. New songs were written and shared. Stories were created and told.

The children were the center of attention, with a gaggle of admirers at every turn. Because the Fae were so long-lived, they tended not to have many children, and newborns were a rare treat. That was a lesson the Fae had brought with them to Earth from their home planet, where they had come close to an ecological disaster due to overpopulation.

Even the seasoned offspring from the past few years captured their fair share of admiration and gifts.

The Fae had learned their lesson well and had heeded the warning even tens of thousands of years later on a different planet. It was far more important for the group to have nearly limitless resources than it was to have large families.

The party was probably far more fun for the Fae than for Davol and Chedrick, who sat on the sidelines talking with Faerie elders, enjoying those of the Faerie's fine foods that humans could eat, and relaxing.

Acorn stayed nearby, talking excitedly of the gestation, and how Flit had progressed in the five months since she hatched. Every time he turned around to find her, she was firmly attached to Chedrick's leg, standing on his shoe and clutching his trouser leg. Flit's left antenna kept drooping into her field of vision. She was constantly pushing it back into place or flipping her head to move it out of the way.

"Looks like you've found a friend," Davol said with a laugh.

***

Finally, late on the third day. Davol went to the Matriarch to thank her for the invitation; the honor bestowed on him, the wonderful event, the fine time, and the excellent food and drink. Chedrick stood nearby, with Flit on his right shoe. She seemed to prefer his right side for some reason.

Davol turned to Acorn, thanking him for the same things, and said "We really have to go now. Thank you again, old friend."

At that moment, Flit flew up to Chedrick's neck, holding on for dear life as though she would never let go.

Acorn gasped! "She flew! She actually FLEW! Her first flight was to you, Chedrick!"

Chedrick just stood there with a small Faerie on his neck and a huge grin on his face.

After saying their good-bye's and thank you's throughout the camp, the two friends departed for their forest home, to catch up on their sleep.

Episode 8—Trust and Believe

Some days later, deep in the woods, Davol looks from his lunch and asks Chedrick, "So, boy, how was it Traveling on your own?"

"It was fine, sir. I had no problems with it. Did I do everything correctly?"

Davol gave a little laugh. "Well, you made it there, you made it back, and you're sitting here now having lunch with me. It appears that you did everything perfectly.

I do have a question for you though, boy. If I were to ask you to Travel to the far side of the world, say, ten years into the future, do you think you could do that, boy?"

"Yes. I'm pretty sure I could, sir. You've taught me well, Davol."

"And what if I asked you to Travel out there," Davol said, pointing upward. "What if I asked you to Travel to the dark places between the stars, further than the eye can see, further than the mind can fathom? Could you do that, boy?"

"I'm not sure, sir. I don't know if I could do that."

"Why not, boy? What makes you say that you can't do that?"

"Well, sir… It's just that, well, it's so far."

"So. It's the distance that bothers you, is it, boy? What if I changed my request so that you had to travel to the treetops in that direction? Could you do that?"

"Oh. Of course, I could, Davol."

"So, then, it's not a matter of you wondering if you were able to Travel, then, is it?"

"No, sir. It's not. I can Travel."

"Then, what is it, boy?"

"Well, it's, it's just that it's so…. It's so very far away, and it's unknown to me."

"Aha!" The Wizard proclaimed. "So, it's not about the traveling, it's about you not being sure of your capabilities."

Chedrick looked sheepishly at his feet. "Yes. I suppose that's so, sir."

"Do you remember me talking to you once about learning to trust?"

Still looking down, Chedrick replied, "I'm not sure, sir. Perhaps if you told me again?"

"As you know, boy, our mind is our most powerful tool. I have trained you to use your mind in ways that most men will never know. In order to continue to grow in your powers and abilities, you must continue to believe and trust that, that which you do, that which you think, and that which you feel, is real. It has the ability to affect others, and indeed, to change your world. Remember this always, boy. The more you believe, the more you'll be given to believe, and the more you trust, the more you will be given to trust. I cannot begin to tell you how very important it is. First and foremost, you must believe in yourself."

Davol's attention returned to his plate. After several bites, he looked up at Chedrick.

"I believe it is now time to take another journey if you are so inclined. We will not take our bodies with us on this Travel, for they would not survive where we are going."

Chedrick looked up from his shoes with a glint in his eye. "Where are we going, Davol?"

When Davol is amused, a huge, easy grin appears on his face, his bright blue eyes contract slightly, and delightful crow's feet appear at the corners of his eyes. When Davol smiles, he smiles with his whole face and radiates joy from his very essence.

Davol was grinning a very big grin.

"Why, to the very place I just asked you to go," he said with a big smile.

"There is a planet that I know of that floats all alone among the stars, with only its own sun for company. Longer ago than either of us can imagine, its sun and seven planets were ripped from the company of their neighbors, to float alone in space for eternity. In the process, six of the planets were destroyed, leaving a vast cloud of debris in their place. This planet, innermost of the seven, survived, along with its sun, and the two of them have been traveling through the darkest heart of space alone, and together, for eternity.

Not even the Star Brothers know of this planet. It is inhabited by a species that may appear very strange to you. They are like dark brown, leathery balls, covered with tough, thick plates that sprout short, stiff grey hairs on their surface. They have no mouth. They have no arms or legs. They have no eyes. With a little difficulty, you could fit one into a bushel basket. I have chosen to call them Brobdingnagians, and to call their world Brobdingnag. They are among the most intelligent beings in the universe. They are completely telepathic. They are so telepathic that, while each individual has their own personality, together, they form a hive–mind. A single mind for the whole planet. Each individual carries the memory of every other individual who has ever lived. No knowledge has ever been lost, only gained and added to by the experiences of each new generation. There is no discord among them, and because of the way they live, their planet is pristine and beautiful. It is one of my favorite places to go when I feel I need to relax and think.

Ready, boy? Then, follow me!" Davol winked out of the forest.

Caught off guard, Chedrick was a few moments behind his mentor but had no problem finding him in the vastness of space.

"See, boy! You did just fine on your own. I knew you could, but you needed to prove it to yourself."

Brobdingnag was indeed beautiful. It was pristine and untouched, with nary a building or road to be seen. The natives lived in harmony with the planet as it was created. Its distant sun illuminated its landscape with a reddish-golden hue, casting soft shadows beside the low rock outcroppings. Nothing seemed to grow taller than Chedrick's knee. The terrain was slightly hilly, with a profusion of rocky patches. There were plentiful stretches of pale green plants that covered the ground like grass, but were nothing like grass. The rocks were all covered with patches of vibrant colored growths something like the lichens Chedrick had seen on some rocks in the forest at home. In the far distance, he could see low mountains. There was only the slight sound of the wind that played upon his ears as he stood there.

"Where are the Brobdingnagians, Davol? I don't see anything."

"Turn around boy. She's right behind you."

Startled, Chedrick spun around to discover that he had manifested almost on top of a Brobdingnagian.

"She? How can you tell?"

"On Brobdingnag, it's quite easy, my boy. All Brobdingnagians are female."

"But, then, how do they…?"

"Just because things work a certain way on earth, does not mean that they work that way on other planets, my boy. There are no male Brobdingnagians. Never have been. On this planet, things work very differently.

Brobdingnagians are another species that have a very long life span, measuring thousands of Earth years. They have no natural predators, and their death rate is extremely low. As a result, reproduction is very low on their species' agenda, and because they are all linked in a hive mind that never forgets, individual survival is relatively unimportant, except to the individual.

If you watch this one, we'll call her Anne, closely, you will notice that she is very slowly, almost imperceptibly, rolling across the ground. What you don't see is that, where ever her body touches the ground, those little stiff, short hairs between the plates of her body, insert themselves into the surface of the ground. They are actually hollow tubes, and they extract nutrients and moisture from the plants and soil near the surface. What you also don't see are the nearly invisible pellets excreted from those hairs that are on her sides and top. In this way, Anne, and those like her, draw what they need from the living soil, enriching it as they pass, and move on, leaving everything unharmed and in perfect harmony.

Perhaps once in 100 years, Anne will deposit a tiny egg into the soil, then roll away from it without a thought. In fact, she is totally unaware that it has happened. The eggs only survive in the soil for a fortnight.

There are tiny white worms that live in the soil. As these worms eat their way through their loamy realm, occasionally they will come across and consume one of Anne's eggs.

The eggs of Anne and her kin have very hard shells, so hard they usually cannot hatch unaided. When the worm consumes the egg and the egg passes through and returns to the soil, most of the hard shell has been dissolved, but the egg itself remains viable. It is the eggs that have passed through the worm that may sprout and grow.

A young Brobdingnagian begins life looking much like a plant."

Davol pointed out a low shrub with a brown bulbous top the size of an apple, growing near their feet. "There's one there. In a few more decades, if it is not crushed by Anne or one of her kin during their ramblings, it will absorb its roots, leaves, and stem, assume its adult form, and begin its long, leisurely, intellectual life as an adult Brobdingnagian.

But that's not all, boy. As the worms move through the soil, they lay their own very tiny eggs. As Anne and her kind roll along and feed, they occasionally ingest the eggs of the small white worms. The eggs require a certain element that is very rare in the soil of Brobdingnag in order to quicken and grow, but there is a special organ within Anne that produces exactly that element and stores it in a small pouch within her body. The ingested eggs are diverted to that pouch, where they are quickened by the special solution. Once quickened, the eggs pass back out of Anne's body into the soil, where they hatch and grow."

Davol turned toward Chedrick, and with a sly wink, said. "See you at home, boy!" and winked out of Chedrick's sight and perception.

The old Wizard was squatting next to their cold campfire, stirring the ashes to prepare a new fire, chuckling quietly to himself, when Chedrick appeared a few moments later.

Without looking up from his task. Davol said, "See, my boy! I knew you could do it! And now, you know it. too!"

Chedrick had nothing to say. He found a few twigs to help start the fire, then brought over a couple of larger sticks to feed the tiny flames.

Episode 9—A Small Sacrifice

"Davol, I'm confused," Chedrick blurted out one quiet afternoon. "When we go to the villages and towns, we find the Old Believers, the Druids, we find the Catholics, we find many other groups, each with their own special priest's clothing, their ceremonies, their rites, and their songs. They worship one or many Gods, in many different ways.

Why are there so many religions? Which one is right, Davol?"

"Oh! Good question, boy, and one that will never be answered to universal satisfaction!" Davol chuckled.

"Each group has its own closely-held ancient traditions, and, to them, those traditions are always faultless and perfect."

In Atlan, it was our understanding that religion of any sort was a way for people to shift the responsibility for things they did not understand to some Divinity outside themselves. There is some good in it, as both you and I know the power of our minds, and of intent.

When groups assemble with the same intent and focus, it can be quite powerful and can make changes in the material world around us. On the other hand, it removes personal responsibility when things are not going well.

Religion can be quite a seductive thing, both for the participants and for the clergy. For the participants, it offers a safe place within their own minds and community; a comfortable place where things are familiar and in order, and they feel protected and nourished.

The problem with religion is that there must be leaders, and when there are leaders, greed will eventually appear, and an ever-growing quest for power and wealth will follow."

"The answer to your question, my lad, lies within each person's heart. If you are comforted by giving credit for the good things and blame for the bad things to some external deity, then religion is for you, and you should choose the one that feels the most aligned with your heart and your beliefs.

If, on the other hand, you are willing to accept that every person has great powers within them, and the ability to use those powers to change the world around us, then religion will be very uncomfortable for you. If you choose to believe that Life, in all of its forms, is sacred, then we must agree that WE are sacred WE are Divine.

When we OWN our Divine nature, we unlock our native powers that religion often masks or forbids. Miracles become second nature to us. We are able to heal others with our intent, and tell when another needs help before they mention it, and more."

"Thank you, Davol. That makes a lot of sense to me."

Davol continued, "In the earliest times, religion began by honoring those things that either supported life or threatened it the powers of sun and rain, the plants that gave us food, and the animals that threatened our existence, or made it better. These things were elevated because they were seen as being more powerful than we believed ourselves to be. Over time, ceremonies grew up to support the beliefs, and religions were born. There were those who discovered that they could use the power that religion offered the gods to enrich their own lives and increase their power over others by insinuating themselves between the worshippers and their gods. This was the beginning of the priesthood and of organized religions.

Because it is so intimately connected with life itself, blood has been used as the ultimate sacrifice in many religions over time. The blood of animals, and their lives, were often offered to the gods, but the most valuable of blood, and lives, were humans, and among the most valuable of human lives were those of the very young, and those of one's enemies. The absolute most valuable blood sacrifice of all, though, was one's own blood.

It's time for another little journey, my boy. I'm going to take you to the other side of this world, a few hundred years ago, to visit a brown-skinned people known as the Olmecs. We will be observing a man called Chi-ten Nehwha, a priest-king of that society, as he performs a public act of devotion to nourish his gods and benefit his people."

By now, Chedrick is quite familiar with Traveling, and in the instant that he nodded assent, the two friends found themselves hovering near the platform atop a stone pyramid, surrounded by jungle.

Standing on the platform with them was a short, stocky man. He was powerfully built, and except for an ornate loincloth and body paint, was without clothing. Across his shoulders, was draped a decorative feathered cape of intricate design and brilliant colors, and around his neck, a feathered and beaded necklace with a disk of pure gold upon which was mounted an effigy of a man carved from green stone. In front of him was a short stone altar laden with a length of thorny vine, an ornately carved ceramic cup, an obsidian needle, a shell containing smoldering herbs, another shell from which the end had been removed, and a fan made of brilliant blue and red feathers.

At the base of the stepped stone pyramid, a colorful throng had gathered in the warm, moist, jungle morning, after a full moon early in the spring, to witness and participate in Chi-ten Nehwha's supplication to the feathered serpent god. This was the day that the priest-king would offer his own blood for the good of his people. This was the day that he would entreat the gods for successful planting, rich harvest, and abundance for his people.

Between the last full moon and this, many enemy soldiers captured expressly for the purpose during forays into the jungle had been sacrificed to the many Olmec gods, but today would be the ultimate sacrifice, the sacrifice of the priest-king's own blood.

Chi-ten Nehwha stepped up to the low altar. The last evening, he had sat with several other priests, and with much chanting and singing, had drunk deeply the juice of a sacred jungle vine that allowed him to see and commune with the spirit world. He picked up the shell with no end, and, turning to each of the four directions, played a blast from the horn to attract the attention of the gods.

The crowd fell silent.

He picked up the shell with the smoldering herbs that numbed his body but enhanced his communication with the other side, the realm of the spirits, and the feathered fan. Fanning the shell and its contents, the embers within it glowed brightly and sent up a thick cloud of smoke from the sacred herbs in the shell, purifying and cleansing all that it touched. With the smoldering shell in one hand and the fan in the other, he bathed his whole body in the cleansing smoke. He paid particular attention to the area under his loincloth.

When he was finally satisfied that he had been cleansed, he put down the shell of smoldering herbs and the fan. Calling loudly to the Feathered Serpent God, Chi-ten Nehwha bellowed, "Behold the gift I bring to you!"

Grabbing the obsidian needle from the altar, he reached under his loincloth with his other hand, and with one swift jab, pierced his genitals. Moving the loincloth to one side, and proudly showing his pierced genitals to the crowd, he withdrew the needle and picked up the thorny vine. Inserting the vine through his new piercing, he grabbed each end, and rapidly drew it back and forth through the ever-growing wound, causing copious blood flow.

Chedrick winced, but there was a roar of approval from the crowd below.

Removing the vine, he picked up the ornately decorated ceramic cup and held it under his dripping manhood until it filled to overflowing, spilling his blood onto the altar of the pyramid. Holding the cup aloft, he repeated his prayers to the Feathered Serpent, that his tribe might prosper, that crops would be good.

Then he collapsed.

Four lesser priests quickly gathered him up and led him to a less-public recovery area.

Chedrick was totally speechless.

"What you have just witnessed was a very sincere and

sacred ceremony," Davol said. "In its own way, and within their tribal belief system, it had exactly the import of a high mass given by Saint Augustine, first Bishop of Canterbury, for King Aethelbert and Queen Bertha.

So, my boy, I will answer your initial question by giving you another question. Which one of these ceremonies is more sacred? Whose gods are real? And whose are imagined? When you find that answer, please let me know, lad. I have wondered for many years."

With that, the two winked out of existence from the jungle pyramid…

… and found themselves…

…standing just outside a shallow cave, high in the highest mountains Chedrick had ever experienced. The sun was just rising and the colors of the sunrise touched the snow here and there with exquisite beauty. There was deep snow all around them, and total silence embraced them.

The view was extraordinary. Everywhere there were mountains so tall they challenged credulity, and valleys so deep they seemed endless.

All was white.

All was pristine.

Everything was beautiful.

Episode 10—Lo Ming Lao

"Where are we, Davol? How did we get here? Where is 'here?'"

"We are high in the Himalayan mountains, Chedrick. They are the highest mountains on earth. We are here to visit a holy man with no gods. His name is Lo Ming Lao, and he practices the Buddhist belief system."

"I've never heard of the Buddhist belief system, Davol. What is that?"

"Buddha was a holy man from this part of the world. Like you and I, he learned the power of awareness to direct not only the material world but more importantly, the internal world the world of the mind. His followers do not see him as a god, but rather as an example to be emulated. They are people of peace, and of peaceful ways. Many, such as Lo Ming Lao, have spent countless days, even months, tucked away in caves such as the one we're standing in front of, alone with their thoughts, meditating.

If you look closely at the snow in front of the cave. You can see footprints leading away from it. Let's go see what Lo Ming Lao is doing."

As they followed the footprints through the snow, Chedrick was completely absorbed in the beauty of the tall mountains and deep valleys that surrounded them. After walking for a half-hour, Chedrick realized something.

"This trail we're following, Davol. He's not wearing shoes and it's very cold and there's snow on the ground. How does he do that?"

Davol chuckled. "Look down our path a few rods, boy. Over on the right, on that big rock."

Chedrick followed Davol's instructions and was astonished to see a nearly-naked man sitting on the very edge of a large rock overlooking a frightful precipice at his feet. A small pile of faded saffron-colored cloth lay on the rock beside him. Although they stood and observed for quite some time, the man on the rock never moved.

"I'm going to move us forward four hours in time," Davol said.

In a blink, it was so. The sun had definitely moved in the sky. Still, the man sat, motionless on the edge of the abyss.

Finally, the still figure began to move. Chedrick noted that the man tipped his head first towards the right shoulder and toward the left. He then turned his chin first to the right then the left and bunched and released his shoulders. Finally, he stood and thoughtfully donned his light robe. When he stood, Chedrick noticed that all of the snow on the rock around where he had been sitting had melted.

"What was he doing? Why did he sit so long without moving? Why is he not cold?"

"Let's spend a little time with him, boy. There's a lot more to this man than you might think.

Lo Ming Lao has just spent nearly a month in that little cave, clad only in his thin robe. He was meditating the whole time. His mind was freed from his body, but the body was protected from the cold by his mental strength.

What you just witnessed, while he was sitting on that rock, was the reintegration of spirit and body.

In a short time, he will begin the two-and-a-half-day journey to the temple where he lives. He is highly revered as a teacher, second in earthly power within that community.

In a week's time, there will be a major ceremony held there. This sacred ceremony only occurs every few years, and monks are traveling from very far away to participate.

He also oversees a school where young girls are trained to be Buddhist nuns. He will go there first, then on to the temple."

Davol and Chedrick followed the old monk as he walked, barefoot, through the deep snow of the high mountains.

Shortly before midday, the monk stopped and studied

some other tracks he had found in the snow. Quickening his pace, he veered off his course and began following those tracks. When Chedrick looked at the tracks he was dumbfounded.

"Davol! What manner of beast has tracks like these? It leaves prints like a man, but these are three times the size of my feet, and big claws like a bear!"

"My boy, there are many beasts and beings that most men know nothing of. These are the prints of a beast the locals know as a 'Yeti.'"

"A Yeti, sir?"

"The Yeti is a cousin of mankind. Yetis are nearly twice my height, immensely powerful, and possess great strength in their arms and legs. They have long white fur over their entire body and long, strong claws. They are quite intelligent and very clever at avoiding being seen. They are very private beasts, and are very rarely seen by Man.

Let's follow the monk's trail and see what he finds."

They had fallen a couple of minutes behind the monk while they had stopped and conversed. Traveling along at about the pace of man would walk quickly, it was only a minute or so before they crested a small snow-covered rise.

"Davol! Is that a Yeti?"

There, not 20 feet away, was the diminutive Lo Ming Lao confronting a Yeti twice his height. There was blood all over the disturbed snow around the Yeti, and a few scraps of colorful cloth scattered here and there in the crimson-stained snow. The Yeti's face and arms were also stained with fresh blood, and the lower part of a tiny leg and shoe lay on the snow.

From their positions and postures, it became evident that this blood-covered, sharp-toothed beast was actually cowering before the old monk.

Chedrick tuned in telepathically to their conversation, hearing the foreign language in his head as English.

"Brother Yeti," the old monk was saying.

"Namaste, Brother Yeti. We honor you and your people. We share our mountains with you, but we have warned you many, many times, that you are not to harm our people. You have killed one of my students again. They are not your food. We had an agreement. Your food is the yak and the other wild creatures of the mountains.

We are people of peace. To us, all life is sacred. We have told you many times that we will not interfere with you, but that you must not interfere with us. Yet, one more time, you have taken a human life to fill your belly.

There are times when one life must be traded to preserve the many. We are now at that point with you, dear brother Yeti. May you reincarnate into a life that encourages you to be mindful of others."

With that, the fragile old monk took a step forward, and, facing the Yeti from a distance of thrice a tall man's height, made certain motions in the air with his hands.

A resounding loud crackle filled the air, as the Yeti's head was thrown violently backward and to one side before bouncing back to facing forward. There was a momentary look of shock in the creature's eyes, as its knees buckled and it collapsed with a broken neck onto the bloodied and trampled snow. Its eyes remained open and surprised, even in death. A tattered and bloody scrap of cloth protruded from under one hairy arm, and one hand almost touched the half-eaten leg.

Chedrick stood in silence for a moment, unable to believe what he had just witnessed.

Silently, his eyes sought Davol's.

Lo Ming Lao turned and continued on his journey as though nothing had happened, adjusting his path to once again direct himself to his original destination, the monastery.

"What did he do to the Yeti? How did he do what he did to the Yeti? I thought you said these were peaceful people?"

"You see, Lo Ming Lao understands the use of energy to affect the material realm better than most people in the world. He used his Chi, his life force energy, to suddenly cause the Yeti's head to swivel and twist forcefully in a way that caused a small bone in its neck to splinter and break. That fracture instantly cut off all the signals from the Yeti's brain to its body, causing its heart, lungs, and muscles to immediately stop functioning. He broke its neck. Its death was necessary to stop the predation of the young women who are studying to become nuns. The death was swift and almost completely painless. It was performed mercifully, and once completed, needed no further words or action."

Still stunned, Chedrick looked to his friend for more guidance.

"There is a Buddhist legend. In the story, there are fifty bodhisattvas, enlightened beings, on a ship and also a thief.

The captain of the ship, who was enlightened, reads the mind of the thief and sees that he's planning to kill the fifty bodhisattvas so that he can take possession of their ship. To prevent this, the captain kills the thief, as it's the only way to prevent the other killings from happening.

According to the story, the motivation for the captain's act was compassion, so the thief would not suffer the bad karma of killing fifty bodhisattvas. Thus, the act was meritorious."

"What do we do now, Davol?"

"We follow the monk, boy. The most important lesson is yet to come. Move us forward two day's time in this monk's life, lad. You've seen me do it. You can do it too! Move yourself, but take me with you."

In a twinkling, the scenery changed. No longer were they at the top of the mountain, looking down on the valleys. Now they were on a minor peak below the top of the higher mountain, at the highest point in one of the valleys that they had been looking at from above.

Episode 11—Every Ending…

Lo Ming Lao walked on through the deep snow, still barefoot, still unaffected by the cold. For him, this journey, like every journey, was an opportunity to meditate. Ahead, at a short distance, was a cluster of white buildings crowned with red roofs, with a scattering of golden trim and gilded statues that glimmered in the waning sunlight. The central building was more than twice as tall as the surrounding structures.

Brightly colored flags of crimson, emerald green, sapphire blue, gold, and snow white were festooned everywhere, from piles of rocks to parapets, to poles stuck in the snow and back to piles of rocks. Each flag had a bold symbol emblazoned on it. Some flags had illustrations and lines of text in a foreign tongue. Everywhere Chedrick looked were long strings of colorful flags, strung like low-lying cobwebs many layers deep, lined with intriguing flag dewdrops. It was a veritable visual cacophony of flags and color.

Lo Ming Lao plodded on, following his solitary path, and oblivious to the familiar surroundings. He was deep in walking meditation as he was on every such journey, and his body was automatically finding its way back home. He would arrive at the monastery when he arrived at the monastery.

He did not remain a solitary traveler for long, though. As soon as his form was spotted by those at the temple, there was a flurry of red and saffron colors against the snow, as a welcoming party hurriedly gathered and rushed out to greet him. The ubiquitous local dogs happily led the way, barking their excitement to the world at large.

It took quite a while for the first dogs to reach him, and the foremost of the welcoming Lamas was a bit longer in arriving.

"Ming Lao, my friend, it is good to have you home,"

Lopsang said as he embraced his friend and affectionately touched foreheads in greeting. "Let us escort you back to the Monastery. Butter tea awaits, and some Tsampa. It is time to break your fast."

As they walked, other monks arrived and joined the party. A small group surrounded Lo Ming Lao. Two of the younger ones took his elbows, acting both as escorts and support for the aged High Lama. From the time he had left the Monastery, a little over a month ago, Lo Ming Lao had not eaten anything but snow.

As they got closer to the temple, they passed other small groups, who stood aside on their path and nodded their heads in respectful homage and deference to Lo Ming Lao.

He was, after all, the second-highest ranking Lama in their community.

Arriving at the Monastery, Lo Ming Lao greeted those who welcomed him, then excused himself to return to his Spartan quarters to meditate and pray, eat and sleep.

In his absence, the temple had seen a flurry of activity in preparation for the upcoming ceremony to be held in only two weeks' time. The brightly-colored space inside the temple had received fresh coats of paint, and every speck of dust had been painstakingly cleaned from floor to ceiling by dedicated monks and devoted locals.

Davol told Chedrick, "This ceremony is only held in this temple once in many years, and monks and Lamas from far and near will be coming to participate. A different temple hosts it each year, and this is the year for this temple. Some are even now making their way across the countryside to attend this event. Let us move two weeks into his future, boy. You know how to do this."

Chedrick made the necessary mental shift, and the two were two weeks in the temple's future. Colorful banners had multiplied everywhere, and monks and Lamas in their finest regalia stood around in groups and small clusters. Far and wide could be heard intoxicating, deep melodious chants, the bells, trumpets, and singing metal bowls of the Tibetan Buddhist faith that overflowed the monastery and filled the quiet valley.

In preparation for the following day's ceremonies, Lo Ming Lao had spent the night in meditation and prayer, all the while forming small but beautiful colorful geometric sculptures created, in the ancient tradition, from colored Yak butter, as offerings to be presented to the seated Buddha statue that filled the tallest part of the temple from floor to ceiling and lit up the room with its gilded presence. It had been carved from wood over a hundred years earlier, and the monks of the temple and the devoted locals had lovingly covered it from head to toe with layer upon layer of gossamer gold for generation after generation. The gold represented the purity of the Buddha. It was called by the locals, the "Buddha as tall as the sky."

For several hours, Lamas and monks, dressed in their finest brightly colored regalia chanted while the horns, as long as three men laying head to foot, were blown. A row of very large drums held aloft on poles were played as accompaniment. Chimes, smaller shell trumpets, and the famous Tibetan metal singing bowls completed the ensemble. At times it seemed like disharmony, but still, a very pleasant one.

Finally, it was time.

Lo Ming Lao, who had spent the entire night preparing himself and his butter offerings, and had spent the entire morning in prayer, knelt in front of the seated Buddha in meditation and prayer while the monks and the audience chanted.

As he prayed and performed the rituals, the room slowly, almost imperceptibly, filled with an otherworldly golden light, and around Ming Lao, like so many multicolored sprites dancing in the air. Bright lights of every conceivable color came into existence, weaving in and out in an intricate dance with one another, becoming ever brighter and stronger. It was the most beautiful display of light that Chedrick had ever seen, and his entire essence was tingling with the energy of what was occurring.

"What's happening, Davol? I've never seen anything like this!"

"When Lo Ming Lao offered his butter sculptures to the Buddha, he also offered himself. His offer was accepted, and, because of his many years of Buddhist practice and sacrifice in an effort to ease suffering for all other creatures, in his death he has become a light bodied being. His essence no longer needs his body or any material form. He has become a halo of pure light.

Watch what happens next, boy."

The chanting in the room continued as this miracle occurred in front of the assembled monk's eyes. Most of the monks could not see what happened next, but Davol and Chedrick both did.

Lo Ming Lao's spirit rose gently from the husk that had been his body and entered the statue through the third eye of the gilded Buddha before him. Once he was completely within the statue, Chedrick was astonished to see that he had turned around and was looking at the assembled monks with great compassion and love, from the Buddha's third eye, just above the nose and between the eyebrows.

It had taken many lifetimes, but the spirit that had been Lo Ming Lao had achieved the level of spiritual development known as the "Body of Light". He was immortal now, free from any need for reincarnation. He was now free to assist all sentient beings from his position in the Spirit realm. His uninhabited body remained kneeling before the Buddha, a nearly weightless husk of the man who had knelt there only moments before.

"I – I think that's one of the most beautiful things I've ever seen, Davol," Chedrick said with tears in his eyes. "I never dreamed such things were possible."

Davol turned his essence to face Chedrick's essence and placed both hands on Chedrick shoulders. "Chedrick, dear Chedrick, my boy, this is but a taste of the beauty and rewards of living a life focused on serving and benefiting others."

Four High Lamas rushed into the room, bearing an ornate platform covered in rich fabrics. They set it down next to the husk that had been Lo Ming Lao, effortlessly picked up the nearly weightless body, and set it on the platform before covering it with a gauzy piece of white silk.

The chants in the room had shifted to a prayer for the

dead, as Lo Ming Lao's body was ceremoniously removed from the room.

Davol removed the two of them to the outside of the building. Chedrick found himself to be quite emotional.

"This all started with my question about which religion is the right one, Davol. About which God should be worshiped and how. Here is a man that worships no God, yet lived a life so good that he was able to return to the spirit world forever."

"As I told you when you first asked the question, boy, mankind creates its own gods, while ignoring its own Divinity. Once you recognize and own that all things are sacred, that life itself is sacred, and because you have life, you are sacred; you must then recognize your own Divinity. When you recognize and own your Divinity, what the world calls 'miracles' become a part of your everyday life.

As the Tibetans themselves would say, 'Everything goes on, but nothing is permanent.'

Let's go home now, boy."

Episode 12—The End of Atlan

It was early the next spring, at the time when the mornings held very little frost, and the first green shoots of new life were beginning to poke their heads above the ground of the forest floor. Chedrick and Davol sat by their campfire. They had been up for hours, rising with the sun. Breakfast had been cooked and eaten, and each sat, sated and relaxed, with their cup of creek water, which they sipped from as they chatted.

They spoke of many things, of the trips they had made as Travelers, and the lives and societies they had seen. They spoke of lessons learned, of experiences shared, not as teacher and student, but as comrades and traveling companions.

Suddenly, Chedrick looked up at his friend, Davol, and asked, "What ever happened to Atlan, Davol?"

A look came over Davol's face that Chedrick had never seen there before a look of immense sadness.

"Well, that's a long and a very sad tale, my boy. It's also an extremely emotional story for me to tell, but I will do my best.

"I loved Atlan. I loved it for its history, for its humanity, for its culture. I loved it for its people and their mindfulness. I loved it for its beauty. I loved it because it was home.

We Atlanteans, unfortunately, lived in a bubble of ignorance. Because we were a benign nation, we supposed that all other nations would be benign. Because we were a nation of peace, we made no preparations for war. Because we were a nation of arts and intellect, we were not prepared for barbarians and conflict.

For centuries, our society was based on teaching the precepts of mindfulness, of concern and action on the behalf of others for the benefit of all. Children who would not or could not be brought into that pattern, as they reached adulthood, were sent to Egypt, to live in a colony there. In that colony, Atlantean precepts were not taught, and chaos and brutality ruled.

Over time, that colony developed its own science, developed its own technology, and developed its own philosophies, which were not in concordance with Atlantean thought. There was a great deal of jealousy among the leaders of that colony over the relative abundance and richness of Atlan. That jealousy became so great, and the quest for power so strong, that spies and operatives were sent back to Atlan to learn the secrets of our power grid and our scientific endeavors.

Once they had learned enough of our secrets, the location of the central power core, how to build our silver apple-seed shaped ships that flew through the skies, and how to mount energy weapons on them, the die was cast.

One beautiful summer morning, a cloud of seed ships could be seen approaching from the mainland. At that same time, explosive devices were detonated in regional power centers around the nation and in key buildings in the capital city."

The old Wizard showed his age in this moment, looking like a defeated old man, and openly weeping as he told his tale.

"I have only seen this as a Traveler. I have only seen it once, and once was too much. The seed ships, sent from the colony in Egypt, each with a single pilot and an energy weapon, spread out over Atlan and triggered their destructive beams.

Beams shot from the seed ship's noses. There were two colors. The crimson beams cut through buildings with ease. The blue beams were designed to cut through humans, cauterizing the wounds as they passed.

I can still feel the screams of the masses as their city collapsed around, and on them. Unable to watch the destruction of the city, I loved, I moved my essence to the seashore.

In the city, the carnage was global, and that was bad enough, but on the seashore where the people had run for safety from the collapsing buildings, it was a hundred times worse.

I watched as the seed ships drifted slowly up and down the coastline. The blue beams were on continuously. Where they struck the sand, the sand boiled and turned to glass, and when they struck a person, whatever they touched was severed instantly, and the wound cauterized by the heat, leaving the victim to suffer.

There was one man on the beach that I will never forget. The beam raked across his mid body, angling from the right rib cage to the left hip. The sand boiled beneath him where the beam had touched it. His legs fell on one side of the boiling trench, and his upper body, on the other. His eyes were wide with terror, his mouth open in a silent scream. Even though I was a Traveler, not there in my body, in his final moments of life, his eyes locked with mine, and all the loss in the universe poured through him into me."

"I thought, 'This is the worst thing I've ever seen in my life.' I was wrong.

In the next moment, the Master Crystal, left to us by the Star Brothers, buried deep, deep below the capital city in the heart of Atlan was detonated. Our capital city, Atlan, and everything surrounding it was instantly vaporized. The power grid fed by that Master Crystal, with links around the world, ceased to function. A bright and shiny civilization had died and a new age of darkness descended upon the Earth."

At this point, the weathered old man collapsed in never-ending, heart-wrenching, silent sobs. Chedrick moved to his friend, put his arm around his shoulder, and comforted him the best he could.

BOOK THREE—THE JOURNEY CONTINUES

CHAPTER 22—A Loong Time Coming

"Boy," the Wizard began one night at dinner over their campfire. "Boy, how long have you been with me now?"

"A little more than seven years, I think," the young man answered. "I believe it was Spring, seven years ago."

"And, have you learned much in that time?"

"I have learned so much more than I ever dreamed was possible. I should never be able to thank you enough for all that you have taught me, shown to me, and awakened in me. My gifts and abilities are far, far beyond anything I would ever have hoped or dreamt. Thank you, my teacher, my friend, my wise mentor."

The Wizard continued, "I must agree with you, boy. You are by far the most apt student I have ever taken. And yes, your gifts and your talents are exceptional. Without ego, and with acceptance, realize that you are more than you dare dream. Realize that all things live within your Spirit's grasp, and may be made manifest through your loving will. Love is the key to the door, and the entrance to the universe of all that may be. Enter and claim your power."

The Wizard paused for a moment, surveying the man his student had become. "I believe you are ready."

"Ready? Ready for what?"

"You said that you didn't know how you could thank me. I have a favor to ask of you. A gift.

I want you to deliver a gift to the Mer people. I will not go with you on this journey. This will be your opportunity to show yourself what you have learned. You have nothing to prove to me, but you have everything to prove to yourself. Beyond the forest of doubt and the mists of confusion lies the peace of acceptance and the joy of understanding. Trust and believe, my boy. The more you trust, the more you'll be given to trust, and the more you believe the more you'll be given to believe. Our mind is our most powerful tool."

Chedrick hesitated a moment. Immediately, he began wondering if he was capable of fulfilling such a request. Did he have sufficient knowledge? Did he have the abilities that might be required? Hesitantly, he smiled a nervous smile.

"I will do whatever I can to be of service to you, Davol."

"Actually, my boy, the service you do will not be to me, but to yourself and to the Mers."

"When do I leave, my friend?"

"You'll leave on the morrow, my boy. Come, sit with me, and I will tell you of the journey to come."

Chedrick came and sat next to the Wizard.

"Four day's journey to the south there is a port city called Limentun. You will need to leave tomorrow morning because the ship you must be on leaves in five days. Once you get to Limentun, find in the docks the master of the ship, Enterprise. Tell him I have sent you. He will be expecting you."

"And how shall I pay him?" Chedrick asked. "We have no gold."

"You shall pay him with the strength of your arms and your back." The Wizard chuckled. "Nothing in this world is free.

From there, you will sail a fortnight with him, and he will deliver you to an island in the middle of the sea. You will know the island by the single large mountain, a volcano, that dominates its landscape. At the base of the volcano, you will find the half-hidden entrance to a large cave.

You will enter the cave."

"And where do I go from there?" Chedrick queried.

The Wizard chortled just a tiny bit. "And from there, my boy, your journey takes YOU!"

"And the gift? What is the gift that I will take?" the young man asked.

"It will be made obvious to you what the gift is, and it will manifest itself when the time is right," the Wizard answered, mysteriously. "It's time now for you to pack and prepare yourself for tomorrow's journey.

One last thing, boy. Always remember that whatever happens on this journey, or in your life, happens FOR you and never TO you. Every event in your life, no matter how hard or terrible it may seem in the moment, will always benefit you with knowledge and growth in the long run."

The following morning, both men were up before the sun. Chedrick, because he could not sleep, and Davol, well, because Davol rarely slept past sunrise.

"I think I've got everything I need," Chedrick said, hefting his pack and gauging its weight. "I tried to think of everything I might need without loading up on things I might want."

"I'm sure you've chosen well, my boy. You're very resourceful, and I'm sure you will get by just fine on what you have with you, and your wits. I have great faith in you. Now, you should be leaving. You have a long way to go, and you must be in Limentun before nightfall, four days from now. Travel the main road south until you come to the third fork, the one with the big oak tree. When you come to that fork, take the left branch of the road and follow it faithfully. It will bring you to your goal. Seek out the docks, and find the ship, Enterprise. Locate the Master, and simply tell him Davol has sent you."

The Wizard embraced Chedrick briefly, turned him around, and clapped him on the back with his right hand. "Pay attention to everything, and remember what I have taught you. I will see you again, once you have completed this adventure."

***

Chedrick's solitary journey to the coast gave him a lot of time to think, to review his life from his earliest memories with Firefinger up to this moment. He felt more than a little gratitude for the experiences and opportunities that had set his feet onto this road at this moment. His right hand reached up and unconsciously clasped the soft leather pouch around his neck that held the clay disk, as big around as a plum, and half the thickness of his finger, that was his only remaining connection to his birth parents. It was blank on one side and carried the heart in a circle design impressed on the other. Even in strong daylight, in brightest sun, one could see the blue glow emanating from the design. The clay was cracked around the edges, from where the design had been impressed into the disk.

The two-week sea journey passed quickly. Chedrick's youth, stamina, and strength served him well, as the ship's master kept him busy from dawn to dusk with all the tasks required to keep a trading vessel functioning on an ocean voyage. When it came time to sleep, Chedrick was more than happy to lay his head on his hard, lumpy rucksack. Even though the youth was tall and strong, his muscles complained bitterly at the tasks of the voyage.

Shortly after a fortnight had passed, late in the afternoon, an island appeared on the horizon. It was an island with a single, tall volcanic mountain that issued a wisp of smoke from its tip.

The master silently approached Chedrick from behind. "Gather your things, lad. There lies the end of your journey."

Chedrick rushed below decks to gather his meager belongings. He was relieved to finally find respite from the hard work of sailing, curious as to what his new adventures might bring, and anxious to put his feet on dry land once more.

Late in the day, just before dusk, the ship droped anchor, and Chedrick and his gear were loaded into the dory. Carefully navigating among the jagged rocks in the bay, the boat landed at the only patch of sand to be seen. Chedrick gathered his belongings, stepped off into the shallow water, and thanked the master of the voyage.

"You earned your keep, lad. I'll give you that. Good luck on your adventure." With that, the ship's Master turned his back on Chedrick, waded the back to the dory, and rowed back to the ship.

CHAPTER 23—Into the Fire

It was far too late in the day to begin exploring his new island residence. The skies were clear, the weather was warm, and the stars were bright. Chedrick lay down for a long and well-deserved sleep.

It was not the morning sun in his eyes that awakened him. It was his inner sense of being watched. Without opening his eyes, he scanned his surroundings for potential danger. Sensing none, he cautiously opened one eyelid and discovered a crab the size of his hand, that was poking at his nose with one claw. Moving quickly, he leaped up from the sand while the crab scurried off into the safety of nearby rocks.

The ship's Master had left him with a couple of biscuits of hardtack and a small amount of water. Chedrick gnawed on one of the biscuits, absentmindedly, as he surveyed his new home.

"Davol said that when I arrived here, my journey would take me. I wonder what he meant by that? Where do I begin? What direction do I take?" Chedrick's mind raced on and on, playing "What if" with itself for a few moments before Chedrick realized what was happening and stopped it. "What if" games often lead to worst-case scenarios, and rarely resulted in productive visualizations.

Choosing to walk with his back to the sun, Chedrick began to explore the island. The shore was mostly made of rocks and sand, but higher up the slope was a verdant jungle with abundant life.

Chedrick moved up the slope, finding food and water in the plants and trees around him.

As he continued his journey around the island's perimeter, something to his left caught his eye. There appeared to be a deep, black hole in the jungle's greenery. And there was more.

There was a feeling, a beckoning. It was as though the black hole was calling to him.

Through his years of training with Firefinger, and now with Davol, Chedrick had learned to pay attention to such subtle guidance. Cautiously, he entered the cavern that lay before him. It had the rich, earthy smell of the forest, a hint of warmth even on this sunny day, and a moistness that was not unpleasant.

"Enter," his guidance told him. "Enter, for this is your path."

Reluctant at first, because the cave was completely devoid of light and he had no torch, Chedrick did what he knew he had to do. He walked into the cavern, trusting that his guidance would lead him where he needed to go.

By the time he had gone twenty steps into the cavern, it was beginning to be difficult to see where to place his feet, but still, his inner guidance told him to keep moving forward, to trust, and to act on that trust. He remembered Davol telling him, "The more you trust the more you'll be given to trust, and the more you believe the more you'll be given to believe."

A few more steps and he found himself in total blackness. Well, not quite total. There appeared to be a blue glow that illuminated his path. Looking around for the source of this blue luminosity, he was absolutely astonished to discover that it emanated from him! He was the source of his own light! He had seen this glow around Davol from time to time, but never dreamed that it was something that he was capable of as well.

As his eyes adjusted to this new environment, he was pleasantly surprised to discover that the blue glow was not subtle at all, but was in fact, sufficient lighting to allow for a confident passage through the darkness of the cave.

His inner guidance took him deeper and deeper into the darkness, lit only by his own, ever brightening, luminescence.

Until he turned the corner.

The cavern was enormous beyond words.

"This must've been the heart of the volcano at one time," he thought to himself. The cavern was so large that his blue glow was lost in the immensity of it.

He stood there for a moment, trying to figure out the best way to traverse the vast field that lay before him.

"COME NO FURTHER!" The thought is so powerful that it reverberates in his brain and echoes, as though it were in a great canyon.

"Who are you? What do you want? You dare to enter this space?" The thoughts are very loud and resound in his brain.

Chedrick begins to speak. He answers, but the cave is so vast, and his voice is so insignificant in that vastness. Instead, he beams his answer to the unseen speaker.

"I am Chedrick, madam," sensing the feminine nature of the one beaming to him. "I have been sent on a quest to the land of the Mers, and this is the path I must travel."

Suddenly, there was a soft, orange glow that reflected from the walls of the far end of the cavern.

Chedrick took a step toward it.

"STOP WHERE YOU ARE!" the voice in his head shouted.

Freezing in mid-step, Chedrick could not help but recognize the voice in his head was touched by pain.

"You're injured! I can feel it !" Chedrick thought out loud. "You're hurt! How can I help you?"

There was a rattling and a clanking, the sound of large objects moving, of large rocks tumbling downhill. The shadows cast in the orange glow suddenly seem to have a life of their own as they moved and swayed against the distant cavern wall. Still, no one showed themselves.

"You are perceptive, son of Man. Yes, I am in pain, though I doubt anything you can do would help."

"Although I am, as you say, only a son of Man, I have been well trained in the esoteric arts, including the arts of energetic healing and distance healing. With your permission, may I use those talents on your behalf?"

"Well! You are an unusual human being, indeed. The first inclination of most humans is to hunt and destroy. You have no idea who or what I am, yet your first inclination is to offer help.

I am impressed. Yes, son of Man, you may do what you can to ease my pain but keep your distance!"

Chedrick reached into his inner being, to that place of compassionate caring. Without attempting to direct the energy, he only held in his mind the concept of healing, of balance, of well-being. He felt the familiar rush of energy swirling around and through him. He felt it as leapt toward the unknown recipient, and he felt the relief and release of the tension that accompanies pain, in the recipient's body, as the cause of the pain dissolved, both physically and energetically, into a state of peaceful balance. It was a simple task; one he had performed hundreds of times before. Chedrick felt a reaction of surprise and relief from the unknown recipient.

A shadow, the size of a small hill, visible in the soft orange glow, shifted and separated itself from the dark masses at the far side of the cavern. A jagged, gigantic head turned toward Chedrick, and a glowing green eye fixed him in its razor-like focus.

"You show no fear, son of Man." The thought came booming into Chedrick's mind. "Do you not recognize me? Do you not know what I am?"

The beast raised her head and opened her mouth in a silent roar. "You now see what I am. Will you now take back your healing because of what I am?" The massive Dragon beamed.

"I know exactly what you are," thought Chedrick. "I can see what you are, but I do not know who you are. Fear only comes from the darkness of ignorance, and I am not ignorant.

Healing is a gift to both the healer and the recipient, and such a gift can only be freely given. Once freely given, it can never be taken back. That is the nature of healing and the nature of true giving. I am very pleased that you have allowed me to be of service to you in your pain and discomfort. The shape and nature of your body have nothing to do with it. The healing was offered to the being, not the body."

"You are indeed gifted, son of Man. I know of only one other human who could have done such a thing. You have been sent by Davol loch Namor."

It was not a question.

The magnificent beast continued. "Davol has been my friend forever. He was a friend of my parents and was there the day I first took flight. I owe him more than I can ever say. If he sent you to me, then I will do whatever I can to help you in your quest.

I am the last of my kind. If there were still other dragons alive, I would be queen of the dragons.

I have had many names over the centuries. I have been called a monster, demon, and worse. I have been called Ancient One, Mother of all Dragons, Great Worm, Ouroboros, and Eternal One. For the past few centuries, Mankind has referred to me as 'Loong.'

I rather like the sound of that, you may call me Loong."

"This world will be a poorer place without Dragons, but it is the way of the world, and so it must be.

I clearly remember, a couple of millennia ago when I felt the light that was my last living brother go out in my mind. The volcano that he was living in exploded with such ferocity that even a dragon was consumed. Of all my kind, I am now alone in the world.

You may approach, son of Man, but not too close." Loong beamed to Chedrick in a mode that was gentler and carried with it a tinge of curiosity.

As Chedrick began picking his way across the cavern floor, Loong moved down from the slope she had been perched on. The ancient Dragon's thoughts were loud in Chedrick's head, as though the venerable dragon was speaking from inside him.

Like an aging but agile, oversized, battle-scarred cat, Loong climbed to the top of a mound made from bits of wrecked ships, strewn all around with shiny bits of treasure gathered over the centuries. She circled three times, and, finally finding a comfortable spot, lay herself down, her glowing green eyes fixed upon Chedrick. Her left fang was blunted, the last foot had broken off, who knows how long ago, in some herculean battle. She was missing half of the middle toe on her left, rear foot, and several feet off of her long, spiked tail. The long remaining section slowly swished back and forth as she began to beam her thoughts to Chedrick.

When they were still a hundred yards apart, and Loong was mounted atop the jumbled mound of broken, mossy parts of ancient vessels, the great beast beamed, "That's close enough for now."

"I have lived more thousands of years than you can number. I have seen the rise and fall of great civilizations, of great cities, and of great men. I have seen this world in peace, and I have known a world in war. Unfortunately, there has been much more war than peace in the history of this place.

"When I was young and strong, thoughtless and foolish, I was a messy, rowdy little fire flinger, a terror, and a destroyer of crops and villages. I was a raider of flocks, and hoarder of treasures." The Dragon swirled her tail, indicating the mounds of treasure littering the floor of the cavern.

"Over the millennia, as I observed the effects of greed and thoughtlessness, the pain and the suffering of the many for the temporary benefit of the few, I have changed, and I have mellowed as the centuries have passed. When one lives as long as I have, there is more than ample time for reflection on what is truly important in this world and beyond.

Chedrick, you have a good heart, a clear heart, a heart that hears others. You are mindful of the results of your actions in your thoughts and deeds. You have demonstrated that you have learned in your short life what has taken me the better part of an aeon to learn. Your healing skills have lifted the heavy pain that I have endured for nearly 100 years. For that I am appreciative and in gratitude, I will answer any three questions you choose to pose to me."

There was a stain, a seepage, where her green blood had long oozed from under the edge of a scale. A century ago, a bold sailor, in an act of desperation, thought he could stop a Dragon with a mere harpoon. In a chance happening, the harpoon struck just as Loong arched her back to dive into the depths for a final attack on the harpooner's ship, lifting the edge of one scale just enough for the harpoon to drive home into her flesh. It was in a spot that Loong could not reach, and that harpoon remained embedded in her flesh and had become an infected, painful, and festering wound since that time. With no way to remove it, the dragon had suffered for a century when Chedrick arrived on the scene.

"I was surprised," the Dragon beamed, that, as you first entered my domain, your first thoughts were not of fear, defense, or violence, but of interest and compassion. It is because of this that I let you proceed. Your healing gift is very powerful, indeed. As a token of gratitude, I will give you a Dragon's gift. In all of my long lifetime, I have given this gift very seldom, and only twice, now, to humans. You may ask me any three questions, and I will answer them honestly and completely. A Dragon's trust is rarely earned, but you have now earned mine."

It was Chedrick's turn to be surprised by this great gift. He sat for a moment on an old treasure chest to gather his thoughts.

Looking up at the ancient Dragon, Chedrick said, "I have my first question, Madam Dragon."

Loong arched an eye ridge and tilted her head slightly in reply.

"Madam Dragon, why is there so much violence in the world of Man?"

"That is your first question, son of Man. There is so much violence in the world of Man because Man has forgotten to compete in harmony with one another, and in their greed, they now compete against one another. They have forgotten that when your neighbor wins, you win as well."

Chedrick nodded in understanding. "So, the quest for power and greed is the base cause for the violence in Man's world?"

"This is not only the cause in Man's world but in the material realm altogether. Societies that work in cooperation grow and excel. Those who struggle for power, wealth, or authority invariably fail. The greatest of leaders is always a dedicated servant."

The great dragon nodded almost imperceptibly. "I have told you that I would answer your questions honestly and completely. I have done so. That was your second question. You have one question left."

Shocked by the realization that he had wasted one of his precious questions, Chedrick spent several moments gathering himself and his thoughts. If one had only one question to ask such an august being, what should it be?

"Madam Dragon," Chedrick began, as it seemed to be rather rude to address such a majestic beast in any other way. "Madam Dragon, I have found my third question."

Loong raised herself from the pile of rubble that had once been ships. Like a majestic, lumbering old lioness, she performed an extended, exquisite stretch, first flexing her neck this way and that, then arched her back, with deafening cracks as her ancient spine adjusted itself. Then, one at a time, she stretched her legs and stretched her claws. Finally, she unfurled her mighty wings, scarred and tattered at the edges as the result of many battles over thousands of years, and stretched them before folding them back into place. She picked her way down from the mountain of rubble, past the piles of gems and jewelry, gold and silver, and the occasional leg bone or skull. She approached Chedrick, trailing puffs of smoke as she exhaled.

Finally, she stopped, not 10 feet away from Chedrick. Her head was enormous. It seemed to take up the entire cavern. Chedrick could feel the strong, hot wind of her breath on his face and arms.

Loong chuckled. A deep, rumbling, powerful, and somewhat unnerving experience from such a close range.

"You have, have you? And what might that question be, child of Man?"

"With respect, Madam Dragon, can you please tell me why there is death?"

Chedrick could have sworn that he saw a flicker of surprise in the dragon's eye.

Loong opened her mouth wide, threw back her head, and roared with laughter. The walls of the cavern reverberated and a stalactite fell from the ceiling, crushing a treasure chest.

Actually, it was probably far more roar than laughter, but in Chedrick's mind, it was received as a heartfelt belly laugh.

"In my entire existence," Loong thought aloud, "I have offered answers to fewer than 100 beings. I must say, child of Man, that is the best question anyone has ever asked me."

"You have let me into your mind, and so I know what you know, and I know who your teacher has been and what you have been taught. You already know that our Spirit is eternal, that our bodies are not, and that time and space only exist for those who require them while in physical form. I perceive that you have read books. Think of our existence as a never-ending book written by our Spirit that we discover as we live it, page by page. Think of each lifetime as a Chapter in that book. At the end of each Chapter, we will often find blank space at the bottom of a page, where all has been said, and when there is nothing else to write. Turning the page, we begin a new Chapter.

It is the same book, and it is the same story, but you will find different characters, different situations, different puzzles to solve, and different rewards in each new Chapter. That which we call death is that blank space between Chapters. It is necessary. It enables us to cleanse our mental palates from the last Chapter's flavors before beginning a new Chapter. It also gives us the opportunity to peruse and consider the events and lessons from the previous Chapter before beginning a new one.

That, young human, is the purpose of death. It is not an ending. It is a pause between Chapters in our never-ending chronicle. When we understand this, we lose our fear of death. When we lose our fear of death, we lose our fear of life!"

The great beast beamed a question to Chedrick. "You have told me that you are on a quest to the land of the Mers. What might that quest be, son of Man?"

Chedrick tells Loong of the mysterious mission Davol has sent him on.

There is a long silence in the cavern and in Chedrick's head. Finally, the Dragon speaks, but now, the thoughts are soft, gentle, and almost matronly.

"There is no trail through the cave suitable for humans, but if you pick your way carefully, you will find what you seek." Nodding with her head to her right and behind her, she points out several landmarks that will guide Chedrick on his way.

"See the treasure chest with a corner broken off and the sword falling out? Walk first toward that. After you pass that chest, another 50 paces will bring you to a place where several stalactites have broken and are laying on the ground. In the distance, you will see a broken ship with but one mast, lying against the wall of the cavern where I threw it several centuries ago. Walk toward that ship. If you reach it, you have gone too far.

When you are about 20 leagues away from the ship, look sharply to your right and you will see a small mountain of gold with a single, large ruby on top. Walk past that pile of gold, and you will see a smaller ship next to a large opening in the wall of my cave. Enter that cavern and pick your way through that pathway. It is very important to stay in the main shaft. There are many branches, but stay true to your path. You will know that you have reached your goal when you see the sunrise."

"Yes, Madam Loong. I thank you for your generosity, your courtesy, and your assistance. Just to make sure I have the directions correctly in my mind; I find the second ship, on the right, then straight on till morning?"

Evidently, Chedrick had used his quota of questions, for the gigantic beast had turned her back on him, and was making her way back to the hidden grotto that she had emerged from. The kind, matronly voice in his head added, matter-of-factly, "Oh. And if you touch my treasure, I will eat you."

Chedrick was fairly sure that she was not joking.

Chapter 24—Your Journey Takes YOU!

Carefully, making his way by the light of the strong blue glow emanating from his body, Chedrick vigilantly followed the instructions given by Loong. He immediately spotted the broken treasure chest and sword sitting on a small rise in the cavern floor and headed toward those.

As he climbed the rise, he saw a pile of scattered timbers and a single, lonely mast. The timbers were strewn like jackstraws, spread against the wall of the cavern. Picking his way carefully over mounds of treasure and occasional piles of bones and weapons, he approached the wreckage.

The great beast's words echoed in Chedrick's memory. "When you are about 20 leagues away from the ship, look sharply to your right and you will see a small mountain of gold with a single, large ruby on top. Walk past that pile of gold, and you will see a smaller ship next to a large opening in the wall of my cave."

Chedrick stepped past a very large stalagmite to his right, a stalagmite so large that it had long since merged with the stalactite above, forming a massive pillar from ceiling to floor. As he walked past it, and looked to his right, he saw a massive pile of gold bars. A treasure chest had been thrown carelessly atop the bars, and coins cascaded down, lodging atop and between. A Ruby gem, the size of his fist, crowned the gilt mountain with regal splendor.

Following the Dragon's instructions, Chedrick walked toward the small golden mountain, then beyond it. In the distance, he spotted the second ship and the opening in the wall of the Dragon's lair.

Entering the new cave, Chedrick was immediately struck by a difference in the feeling of the air about him. There is a certain smell associated with a fire-breathing dragon and its lair.

It's not an unpleasant smell, more of a slight taint to the air. A dryness-by-nature, and perhaps a tiny whiff of brimstone. Entering the new cavern, he smelled moistness, somewhat like the forest floor after a rain, but different.

The path sloped downhill, sometimes precipitously so, but overall, the journey was not difficult. There were far fewer stalagmites to negotiate and the moist air felt good to breathe.

After walking for hours, Chedrick became aware of light in the distance. It was not the blue glow that his eyes had become accustomed to, but the golden glow of sunrise.

Chedrick hastened his step, eager to be once more in daylight. The cave had been cold and clammy. He could hardly wait to stand in the sunshine!

There was a rock overhang at the exit to the cave, like an extended eyebrow of stone, hanging with vines that covered half the opening. Stepping through the vines, he greedily turned his face toward the sun… and saw … nothing!

Well, not exactly nothing, but certainly not what he had expected to see!

The warm, golden illumination he had seen in the cave had come from an enormous dome. It was so far across that he could barely make out the far wall in the great distance. The top of the dome rose almost half that far above his head, and the glowing light seemed to come from the walls of the dome itself. There was also a gentle, radiant warmth that warmed his bones, cold from his long night's dark journey.

"You look funny. Why is your skin that color?" beamed into his head.

Chedrick snapped out of his reverie instantly, looking around to see the source of the comment. A young child was squatted down by the edge of the cave, playing in the mud and holding a muddy, squiggly creature between her thumb and finger. Standing up, the youngster gently dropped the critter back into the puddle it had been drawn from. She looked at Chedrick. "Your skin. Why is it that color? Are you sick? Where are your gills? Your clothes are funny. Are you a monster? My mommy told me not to go into the cave because monsters live there. Are you going to eat me?"

"Who are you talking to?" A distinctly feminine energy asked from nearby.

A young woman, clearly mother to the child at his feet, came into view around a rock outcropping to his left, then stopped in her tracks as she spotted Chedrick. It would be hard to say who was more startled.

In the far, far distant past, the Mer civilization had begun as another colony of Atlan, populated by those with a particular affinity for the sea, her ecology, and her life forms. Over time, since the Fall of Atlan, the people had evolved into a slightly different species. Mers had a different skin tone a pleasant, subtly mottled blue-green cast, and slight webbing between fingers and toes. Their heads were bald and shaped slightly differently from land dwellers. There were other, subtle differences as well, such as their ability to withstand the tremendous pressures of the deep sea, and their ability to hold their breath for extended periods, amounting to several hours at a time. Their torsos were larger than land dwellers, to accommodate their larger lungs. They were both verbal and telepathic.

The young woman gathered her wits about her quickly, closed her right hand into a fist, and placed the fist above her heart in greeting. She spoke. "You're a land dweller. I've heard of your kind, but I've never seen one before. I'm Iral. How did you make it through the cave? I've heard that monsters live there."

"My name is Chedrick. I am a land dweller, and I have been sent here on a mission to help the Mers. Am I correct to assume that you are a Mer person? There is indeed a monster in the cave, by the way. I was fortunate enough to be able to get past her, unharmed."

They took a moment to study each other, to take in the differences and note the similarities between them.

"I am a scientist," Iral said. "I came out with my daughter to measure how far our dome has shrunk. Would you like to come back to the University with me and meet my colleagues?"

Davol's words echoed in his mind. "From there, your

journey takes YOU."

"I'm ready. Let's go!" Chedrick replied.

"Lenta! Clean up and get your things. We're going now!"

Chedrick assisted them in gathering their possessions and equipment, then volunteered to pack the heaviest pieces, on their walk back to the city. The hour-and-a-half walk gave them time to talk and get to know one another, while Lenta amused herself with rocks, sticks, and insects they found along the path.

The city of the Mers was spectacular and by far the largest city that Chedrick had ever seen. The buildings appeared to be made of glistening white stone with large openings in the walls to promote natural ventilation within. Some spires reached nearly half the height of the dome roof above them. Everything about the city looked well-groomed and pristine, and there was abundant open space, almost park-like, with abundant walking paths like the one they were on, winding throughout the city. Twice, Chedrick tripped over nothing as he tried to take everything in at once.

"This is the University," Iral said as she gestured toward a complex of sparkling white buildings before them. The University, like the rest of the city, was spectacular.

Except…

Emblazoned above the main entrance, 3 feet across, high above the door was the symbol.

THE symbol.

The very same symbol he had seen all his life on the clay disk he still wore in a pouch around his neck. That same small disc the Raven dropped at the feet of Chedrick's biological father, the farmer, that had been kept by his wife and picked up from the ashes of their cottage, along with the infant, by Firefinger. Chedrick carried it with him in his neck pouch at all times.

Chedrick realized that he had been left behind by Iral. He had been transfixed and lost in thought by seeing the familiar symbol in an unfamiliar place. He hastened to catch up with his guide.

"… founded before the fall of Atlan, when the world

was a far different place. Our city was much larger then. Without the Atlantean power grid connected to it, our own power crystals have been slowly losing power, and as they die, our protective dome shrinks. We are losing more of our city every year to the sea around us. In just a few hundred years more, our city will be gone, and all of our people will be dead. We are trying to find ways to renew our crystals. That is what my group is studying."

Making a sharp right turn at a corridor, she took a few steps forward and entered a room on her left.

Her entrance garnered barely a glance from the room's three occupants, but when the older gentleman who had been writing looked up and realized that she had a guest with her, and that that guest was a land dweller, he gasped loudly, and all activity in the room abruptly stopped.

All attention suddenly was upon Chedrick.

"Well! This is a surprise! Iral, what have you brought us?"

"This is Chedrick. He is a land dweller sent here on a quest that he does not yet know the details of. He has traveled far, over land and sea, and through the cave of the monster to be here. I was collecting samples near the mouth of the cave when he came out from it.

Chedrick, this is Letone, one of my fellow researchers. This is Umbral and Denon; they are two of our student assistants."

Chedrick barely overheard Umbral and Denon whispering excitedly between themselves. He couldn't catch much of it, but he heard 'legend' and he heard 'Li' several times during the exchange.

Letone turned to Iral. "We must inform the regents immediately!"

Letone stood up from his desk so rapidly that he knocked his notebook on the floor and scattered papers around. He stooped to pick them up, then waved his hand at the mess in dismissal and moved quickly towards Iral and Chedrick. "Come on then. Let's go!"

On the short sky-bridge walkway to the regent's offices near the top of a nearby tower, Letone barraged Chedrick with questions, much as Lenta had. He had so many questions and asked them in such a rapid-fire manner that Chedrick had no opportunity to answer even a single one before they found themselves in front of the regent's office.

Letone was still talking as they passed through the doorway.

Camier loch Davaron was of a lineage that could trace their biological heritage to the Star Brothers of ancient times. He was slightly rotund, and quite old, nearing 250 years, but his intelligent eyes shone brightly from his pleasant and kindly, wrinkled face.

That face registered considerable surprise at the moment.

"A land dweller! A land dweller? You've brought me a land dweller? My great, great, grandfather used to tell stories of having seen a land dweller once when he was a child!

Where are my manners? Welcome sir, to the land of the Mers. Sit down, please. What can we do for you? You must be hungry, and tired." Camier gestured to one of his assistants, who scurried off in search of food and drink for Chedrick.

"I have been sent on a mission to the land of the Mers by Davol loch Namor."

"Ah! The House of Namor! I studied House Namor in my history lessons when I was a young student. But that line died out over 10,000 years ago! How is that possible that you have been sent here by a member of the House of Namor?"

Chedrick, by now stuffing his mouth with delicious food and cold beverage, swallowed and put his plate to one side. For the next 10 minutes, he told of his life with Davol and the mission that he had been sent on.

Chedrick had finished speaking. Camier sat silently, staring intently at the young land dweller.

"And what is this mission that the House of Namor has sent you on?"

"I'm really not sure, sir," Chedrick replied. "Davol told

me only that I am to perform a service for the Mers. He told me that 'my adventure would take me.' I'm really not quite sure what that means yet."

Camier sat silently for nearly a minute, deep in thought. There had been a steady stream of Mers, far more than normal daily traffic, that passed by the doorway to the regent's office. Every person who had passed would crane their neck for a view of the land dweller. A steady murmur of subdued but excited chatter could be heard from the hallway.

"Would you care to see a little more of our city?" Camier finally broke his silence.

Though he was tired, but now fed and somewhat rested, Chedrick eagerly agreed.

Camier signaled to members of his staff, who scurried off to arrange lodging for Chedrick and to spread the word of the land dweller's presence in their community. Gathering a few items from his desk, Camier nodded to Iral, and, together with Chedrick, they headed out for a short walking tour of the University campus and beyond.

As the trio made their way through the corridors of the University building and made their way toward the exit, they were unaware of how every opening in the building above and behind them filled with onlookers, pointing and speaking with animation and excitement.

When they left the University grounds and began walking through the city, Chedrick was completely focused on the surroundings, the buildings, and the day-to-day life of the Mers. The Mer people were just as fascinated with Chedrick.

Everywhere they went in the city of the Mers, there were pointing fingers, whispers behind hands, and eyes that had looked startled. As he was the only land dweller in view, he attributed the furor to his unique appearance in this strange land. He was most definitely the center of attention.

Little did he know of the ancient prophecy that spoke of a land dweller, bringing with them the Li the quickening spark that would reignite their city's failing power crystals, the quickly-dying, single energy source for the energy dome that kept the sea at bay and the Mer people alive.

Chedrick did not know of the legend, but as he walked through the city of the Mers, unspoken hope gleamed in the eyes of all who saw him.

Chedrick suddenly realized that Camier had been speaking to him all along, acting as a tour guide in pointing out various landmarks within the city.

"And next, sir, I'd like to take you to see this city's power station, where the crystals, which provide the power for our entire civilization, are kept."

They walked on for another fifteen minutes, toward the center of the city. There, in front of him, was a low-slung, square, sparkling white building with a low white dome that seemed to flicker in and out of existence, even as Chedrick watched.

CHAPTER 25—But Fate Has Its Way

Stepping in front of Camier and taking charge of the situation, Iral told Chedrick of the Star Brother's technology harnessed within the gigantic crystals. How, at one time, they were part of a planetary energy grid, tied to and fed by the colossal power stations throughout greater Atlan. Even though Atlan had fallen many thousands of years before, the crystals had continued to supply power to the city, though at an ever-diminishing rate, as they consumed themselves. They were weakening rapidly. Their days were numbered. The city of the Mers could last no more than a few hundred years longer before the crystals died completely and the ocean reclaimed the city.

The group turned slightly right, off the pathway they had been walking on, and onto a somewhat narrower cobblestone path, beautifully set with intricate designs made from small colored pebbles worn smooth by many centuries of foot traffic. The grounds of the power center, like the rest of the city, were park-like, with nary a blade of grass out of place. The path led them slightly downhill, in a gentle curve toward the building. Soon they found themselves standing in a sculpted doorway with climbing vines framing the sides.

Unconsciously, Chedrick's hand crept up for a moment, to the well-worn pouch around his neck. Was it his imagination, or was it becoming warm to his touch?

By now the walkways surrounding the building were crowded with Mers a crowd so abundant that it spilled over onto the greens surrounding the power center. The murmuring of the crowd became so loud that it was difficult to carry on a conversation. The one phrase heard over and over, above the din, was "Li'in."

Iral and Chedrick entered the building, with Camier close behind. A couple of trusted assistants stood in the doorway to keep the crowd at bay.

Chedrick's eyes scanned slowly around the room. It seemed to be a very ordinary room, plain, in fact. There were two remarkable features, however. One was the semi-translucent overhead dome that flickered in and out of existence as he watched. The most interesting part of that was that when it flickered out of existence, instead of seeing the dome above, he saw stars and space.

The other unusual feature of the room was the huge circular hole in the floor. It was as wide across as ten men standing on each other's shoulders. Deep within this hole, standing out strongly in the darkness that surrounded it, was the largest crystal Chedrick had ever seen. It glowed with the same blue light that he had become so accustomed to throughout his life; that vibrant baby-blue light that indicated a deep connection with The Way.

The light was pulsing, almost flickering. It seemed sickly, wan.

As Chedrick leaned over the edge to look at the crystal below, the worn leather pouch around his neck shifted, and it pulled at its thong. Fearful of losing it to the dark abyss below, Chedrick reached up to grab it, then jerked his hand away in surprise.

"It's too hot to hold!" He shouted to nobody in particular. He shook his hand and blew on his fingers to cool them off. "And it's vibrating! It's never done THAT before!"

Still, the pouch pulled toward the crystal.

Harder and harder it pulled...

The red neck thong was just long enough that Chedrick could see in front of him, that the familiar blue glow of the disc within had brightened so much that he could see the heart-in-a-circle through the leather!

...which was smoldering, charring, and burning through!

Almost as though it was happening in slow motion, the disk burst through the charred leather and shot toward the crystal below.

Without thinking, Chedrick leaped from the edge to

rescue the last remaining artifact that tied him to his birth parents…to that cabin so very long ago.

And he fell.

Toward the crystal.

The disk tumbled, seemingly in slow motion, just out of reach, in front of his outstretched hand, accelerating toward the crystal. It shimmered with blue fire almost too bright to look at!

It took only a split second, but that split second seemed like it went on forever.

Exerting every effort, Chedrick stretched his arm out, his fingers grasping the air. He almost had it!

Then, the entire world exploded.

CHAPTER 26—A Beginning in Disguise

Chedrick came to. He was lying on his back on the floor of the power station. He was splayed out in an awkward position with one foot still hanging over the edge of the deep hole that contained the crystal.

Things were different now. Where the power station had been dimly lit by the glow of the crystal, everything stood out in sharp relief. That wonderful, vibrant baby blue flooded the entire chamber. The dome in the center of the roof was solid, strong, and beautiful in its radiance.

Around him, he heard others moaning and moving around as they, too, regained consciousness.

All eyes were on Chedrick as he picked himself up off the floor. All eyes, which had once reflected only hope, now sparkled in open admiration and reverence.

Chedrick turned to Iral, who had opened her eyes and had just begun to move her legs. "What happened," he asked. "What happened?" Iral sat up and looked at Chedrick with tears pouring down her face. "Li'in. You are indeed the Li'in of the legend. You have saved us all. You have saved the city. You have saved our children!" Iral could say no more, but simply sobbed.

Her tears conveyed a lifetime of dread, of fear for the future, and a sudden and absolute end to those fears. It was obvious that the relief was more than she could bear.

When she could speak again, Iral explained to Chedrick that, according to ancient legend, there would come into their city, traveling alone, a land-dweller who would bring with him the Li the sacred seed that much-needed catalyst that would re-ignite the Star Brother's off-world technology. It was that focused and distributed energy from and through the giant crystals in the generating stations that sustained the dome and all of Mer life.

The crystals and their energy had begun winding down, and the off-world science had been lost, at the time of the Collapse the great Darkness that befell the world when Atlan was destroyed. The Mer power centers had lost their ability to self-rejuvenate and had been slowly dying ever since.

The one who legend said would bring that quickening agent, the Li, was called by the Mers, the "Li'in."

Chedrick looked around him, and noted that the people in the room were all sobbing, and hugging one another. Poor old Camier had actually wet his pants because he was crying so hard.

From outside the power center, a great hue and cry could be heard across the city. As Chedrick and Iral stepped outside the door, they were greeted by the largest crowd Chedrick had ever seen, and under the vibrant blue dome above, the cry resounded and echoed "Li'in! Li'in! Li'in!" People began to bow down to him, until, at last, there were none standing. Even Iral, still holding his hand, got down on her knees and bowed to the man who had saved her world.

***

There followed, in the city, four days of nonstop celebration. Scientists who had worked with Iral reported that the dome was rapidly expanding, and that as the boundary passed over buildings long claimed by the sea, the seaweed and other residue from the long time underwater had simply disappeared as it passed beyond them.

The nation of the Mers was once again well, vibrant, and strong.

On the fifth day, Davol appeared.

CHAPTER 27—Homeward Bound

It was on the fifth day of the celebrations, celebrations that seemed as though they would be never-ending. This one was a spontaneous gathering of citizens in the grand Plaza outside the governmental offices. More people were giving speeches, citizens were handing flowers to one another, artisans of all sorts were giving away their wares and the finest Mer chefs were trying to outdo one another in preparing their finest offerings, which were freely given to the crowd.

Chedrick, of course, was the center of attention.

Until…

A vibrant blue vortex, slightly larger than a man, appeared a few feet away from Chedrick.

The Plaza fell silent.

A tall old man, long of beard, with white hair cascading down his back, wearing a light blue robe and cap, and carrying a twisted, blonde, wooden staff with a color-changing crystal mounted atop it, stepped from the vortex. He looked about for a moment, walked over to Chedrick, took him by the arm, escorted him back into the vortex, and they both disappeared.

… And stepped out onto the tranquil shore of an island near the forest Chedrick called home.

"Davol! How good to see you again! But why did you take me away from the Mers like that?"

"Because you had accomplished what you went there to do, my boy. There was no point in staying longer. The Mers no longer needed you. You had performed the function only you could do."

Chedrick asked Davol, "My teacher, my friend; I am sorely troubled. If you have known for tens of thousands of years that I was the one to liberate the Mers from their failing society, and you have had the power all along to end their pain and restore their society, how could you be so cruel as to let it go on for so long?"

Davol replied, "Sometimes we are born to a great challenge a supreme destiny that we have no inkling of, until after it has happened to us.

There are those of us who truly understand The Way, who live it in every moment. We are the ones who walk between worlds, bounce from dimension to dimension, change reality for others with a wave of our hands and heal the sick with a thought.

Some might think that such power would corrupt, but those who can be corrupted will never attain these powers.

Some might think that those with such power would have an obligation to banish all sickness, to ease all pain, but in truly understanding The Way, one sees that, within The Way, there are reasons for sickness, for pain, just as there are reasons for supreme joy."

"It is true that nothing in our life experience ever happens TO us, but only FOR us. Every event we witness or experience carries within it, its own lessons, and the seeds of the opportunity for growth that might not otherwise be realized in that lifetime.

Some, who do not understand The Way, might think that there is far too much to be accomplished in one short lifetime, but those who truly understand The Way know that each lifetime, no matter how long or short, no matter how pleasant or painful, is but a single page in an endless book that each one writes alone, yet all of us study together.

We are immortal, even though our bodies are not. When we lay down one body, we return to the cosmic Oneness of The Way, where all are one, and yet, we still retain the illusion of our individuality. When the time comes to reincarnate, we bring with us the core of our being, our essence, augmented and colored by our latest experiences and most important learning goals."

"Allow me to demonstrate. Here is a portion of food from another time and place. It is called tapioca." Davol first manifested, then handed Chedrick a small bowl with a white, lumpy substance in it. Chedrick looked at it dubiously, and sniffed it several times, looking at Davol uncertainly. "Taste it!" Davol encouraged him. "It's really quite good."

Scooping some of the sticky white paste with his fingers, Chedrick gently touched his tongue to the goo. His eyes lit up and he swiftly scoured the bowl clean and was soon licking his fingers.

"That tapioca is a perfect example of what our Spirits experience after the event we call 'death.'"

Chedrick's face reflected a complete lack of comprehension.

"Pay attention, now, boy. This is a simple explanation, but it can take a lifetime to understand it fully.

When a person 'dies,' their initial experience is dictated by their strong beliefs, if any, in life. Those without strong beliefs may experience a period of being attached to the earth and the people and things they were associated with on this material plane. Those who die suddenly and/or unexpectedly are often unaware that they are dead.

Those souls often manifest as 'haunts' and things that go bump in the night."

"I have found that in death, as in life, perception creates reality. The belief system of the person who dies dictates, to a large degree, what they will first experience when they travel beyond, to the etheric side.

I have sometimes helped 'lost' souls into the higher levels of awareness and acceptance. I once aided a soul who had died 1,200 years before and was completely unaware of its death. That soul had traveled in a limbo of not-knowing for 12 centuries. Because there is no time outside the material realm, this period had passed without seeming exceptional to this soul. This level is confusing and frustrating to the souls, and many will become angry or adamant that the living recognize, and interact with them. When this does not happen, they increase their efforts to be noticed, often becoming troublesome and frightening to humans.

Once a soul moves into the higher levels (and there are

many of these levels), most will continue to 'graduate' into ever higher awareness and Light with less and less need to remain connected to the things and people 'left behind,' and have more awareness of the Oneness of all things and the identity of self as an indistinguishable aspect of The Way."

"So, some people died without knowing they're dead?" Chedrick asked. "How can that be?"

"Many people die in their sleep, or from a blow to the head, or from some other unexpected and sudden cause, as Sarah and little Edwin did. Their conscious mind has no opportunity to grasp the fact that they are dying, and as a result, many of these souls think that they are still alive," Davol replied.

"Do you think my parents know that they're dead?" Chedrick asked.

"Firefinger attended to them after the death and ensured that they knew their condition. He also saw to it that they were assisted in their transition from bodies to not having bodies. They are at peace."

"You've told me a lot about what happens when we die. How do we go about returning to a body?"

"When a soul is ready to return to a mortal form, it reaches an agreement with souls already in mortal form to host the baby and raise the child. It carefully selects attributes of its parents, environment, and society that it will be born into."

The Wizard went on. "When a soul chooses to return once more to the mortal realm as a human, there are decisions to make and 'packing' to do.

Think of it this way, boy. We, as souls, go into our room of possibilities and stand there pondering: 'Since I'm returning to the material realm to learn about (insert your favorite lessons here), I'll need ….' We then proceed to pick our body style and race, our skin color and environment, our parents and siblings, our abilities and disabilities, and much, much more. Like most trips, we are only able to pack so much. The rest of our 'needs' we will have to pick up while on our life journey."

"Wait!" said Chedrick. "What are you saying? You're saying that we pick the bodies that we wear, our parents, and whether we're men or women?"

"Yes. What we pick becomes, in the broader sense, our 'costume.' As we gather together our costume, we begin assuming the energies and attitudes of our new role. Our 'costume' enhances our role and our role enhances the costume. Neither of these things is truly 'us,' yet we appear to be these things while we are in human form. By the time we are born, we are largely 'locked-in' to our character, our costume, and our role."

"So, it's all like being in a play, I guess?"

"Yes, that's a very good way to look at it, boy. I believe you're beginning to understand. When we die, in most cases, we are convinced that our costumes and our characters are who we truly are, and most of us die with our costumes still 'on'. It is these personas these costumes that are stripped from our untarnishable, eternal, and sacred essence in the various levels of existence after death.

Depending on how deeply we identify with our last costume, this can take a LOT of work."

"So, you're saying that I'm really not Chedrick and you're really not Davol?"

"No, I'm not saying that at all. You really are Chedrick, but you are far, far more than who and what Chedrick appears to be. That is one of the reasons I have come to you, to mentor you, and to help you unlock your awareness of who and what you truly are and all that you can become. That which the world refers to as 'Spiritual growth' is never, ever, a matter of growing more. It is always, and only, a matter of limiting less. If each day, you learn to limit less, there will come the day where you will recognize that you have always been, limitless.

That's enough for now. We'll talk more about this later."

***

It rained that night, hard and heavy, all night long, but the morning brought clearing and warm sunlight. Chedrick had dreamed, a very busy dream, but in the morning, he couldn't recall any of it. The boy and the Wizard spent the day in silence.

Not because there was nothing to talk about, but because there was so much to talk about. It was a time for thinking, for reflection. Chedrick gathered firewood and mushrooms and sat on a mossy log that wasn't quite as dry as it appeared. He jumped up and brushed futilely at his now-soaked-through breeches. Returning to camp, he stood with his back to the fire to dry out.

"Oh! You're back. I see you found mushrooms, and some water too, evidently." The Wizard said with a twinkle in his voice. "The mushrooms look very tasty."

CHAPTER 28—Life, the Universe, and Everything in a Bowl of Tapioca

Chedrick jumped back into the previous evening's conversation. He had been rolling it over in his mind all day. "So, if we're not really who we are, who are we?"

"We are, in each lifetime, whoever and whatever we believe ourselves to be, but that is not who we truly are," Davol continued. "In my understanding, the highest level that most souls will reach is best represented by an infinite and multi-dimensional (or non-dimensional) bowl of tapioca."

Chedrick remembered the delicious confection, and once more, absentmindedly, licked his perfectly clean fingers.

"When looking at a bowl of tapioca, at first glance it appears to be a nearly solid mass of translucent spheres with slightly more solid cores, floating in a communal broth. Is that not correct?"

Searching his memory, Chedrick nodded assent.

Davol furrowed his brow slightly and absentmindedly rubbed the spot between his eyebrows with his fingertip for a moment. "In my understanding, that broth could be considered 'The Way.' It is complete with or without the tapioca, but it is created in part as a result of the tapioca's presence.

That eternal broth is something that each core or nucleus is steeped in. One might call it the critical 'Breath of Life,' which makes us more than dust. Without it, we are nothing, but with it, we are All that IS. We ARE The Way.

If we then begin to study both the individual tapioca nodules and the broth, we make some interesting observations:"

Chedrick shifted his position. His pants had nearly dried, and he turned around to face the Wizard.

"If we were to look at each soul as a single piece of tapioca, we would find that the core consists of that particular soul's eternal path and most profound experiences, and the karmic lessons insufficiently learned in previous existences, that have been saved for future study.

This is the core, the most substantial part of the individual grain of tapioca. It is the part that can most accurately be defined as 'us.' From that point, it becomes more and more dispersed as it reaches the outer edges of our awareness, and it begins merging with the oneness of The Way. That jelly-like mass is that soul's acquired wisdom as well as its most recent experiences.

On the outer edges of each orb is an area where information is constantly being exchanged with the universal 'broth' which permeates every 'individual' piece through and through. As a result, we retain our core 'soul' while exchanging, interacting, and modifying who and what we are with the souls and experiences of the entire 'bowl' and with The Way. The Way is ultimately the source and the essence of all being.

As each of us grows, we add to the experience and growth of the entire bowl, making an ever-enriched broth."

"Wow." Chedrick hadn't realized that he had been holding his breath until he exhaled the word. "That is a lot to take in, in one sitting."

"I warned you that it could take a lifetime to fully understand it. Telling you about it is only the first of many steps you must take to fully understand it. There is just a little more that I'd like to share with you. We'll talk more, later."

Chedrick awakened the next morning to the sound of the local squirrels' territorial disputes. It was mating season, and it seemed that each squirrel was determined to define his territory by the sheer volume of his squawks and chirps. Davol was already up and away from the camp. Chedrick rolled up his bed and straightened up the camp, awaiting the Wizard's return.

At midday, Davol came strolling back into their camp. "Perhaps we should finish our discussion from yesterday." The Wizard suggested. Without waiting for a reply, Davol said, "We have just a little bit more to cover for now. Sit down, my boy."

The Wizard began. "When we, as individualized aspects

of The Way, finally come to that state of evolution where we can release the need for experiences and the illusion of existence separate from the oneness of The Way, our tapioca's nucleus dissolves, and ceases to exist as a now-unnecessary reminder of our 'uniqueness.' At that point, we recognize and own our status as The Way, itself. At that point, we become entirely and only the broth, and we serve to nurture all others who have not yet arrived at that point of awareness. This quickens the entire broth and speeds the ultimate enlightenment of the entire bowl. This is what we saw with Lo Ming Lao, when he became a body-of-light being."

"My head is spinning. This is so much to understand. I can see it, but I don't quite understand it yet." Chedrick shook his head as though trying to clear it. "Go on."

"The Way IS balance. The Way can, and has, survived quite nicely for countless eons without the interference of conscious beings. We are unnecessary, yet we are integral parts of the incredible mechanism that is The Way."

Davol finished the conversation. "Every choice we make, and every action we take, creates and enhances, and shapes our personal and our shared reality. You will understand more as you experience more in life."

CHAPTER 29—The Unveiling

Davol hesitated a moment. He gazed at Chedrick, and his eyes softened.

"There is more to it than that, Chedrick. The reason I sent you on the quest to the Mers by yourself goes far deeper than you might think. Your quest was the very reason that I first came into your life. It is the reason that I have spent these many years watching over you and teaching you.

That clay disk that you have carried all of your life was the Li. You were born to be the Li'in. In that moment when your little clay disk touched the Mers' crystal and reawakened it, you were inches away from that sudden surge of power. You have literally touched The Way, and it has touched you as it has never touched another human being. At that moment, Chedrick the boy was destroyed, and in that same moment. Chedrick, Li'in of the Mers was created. There never has been, nor will there ever be again, a human being such as you have become.

My boy, though I can hardly call you that, for, in the years we have spent together, you have truly become a man, I cannot begin to tell you how proud I am of you as both a student and a completed being. You have now learned all that I am to teach you in this lifetime. You have become a great sage, a healer, a magician, and a leader who hears his heart in every decision and action. You stand upright in the power of your own truth. You are all that I might have asked for and more. I am pleased."

"There is nothing more I can do for you now, except to love you as though you were my own son, and I do not need to be in your presence to do that. We have traveled across time and through many realities to arrive here today. You have seen and learned more than any living man. You have seen the lives of many and understood their challenges. You have felt their grief and celebrated their achievements and joys. Always remember that who you are is not what you were. There are no 'wrong' turns in life, only longer, more difficult choices that bring us the lessons we have requested, whether we enjoy the experience or not. When we leave victimhood behind and participate consciously in each event and moment as a student, every journey can become a joy!

Fear is your consciousness confronting the unknown without understanding. The most common human response is to play all of the 'worst-case scenarios' and react to THOSE!

I have taught you that our Spirit is never-ending; that our current bodies are only temporary homes to that unending Spirit. All of the lives we have observed in our adventures together, Gareth Zed, Sarah Bottomly, Chi-ten Nehwha, Lo Ming Lao, even Anne the Brobdingnagian, and all the others; those were all your same Spirit, in different times, in different bodies, with different tools, different lessons to learn, and different agendas for their lives. They were, and are, all the same soul that inhabits your body now. Each one is a chapter in the book of your existence as a Spiritual being, just as you are. In some lifetimes we are destined for greatness and achievement. In some, we are only trying to survive, and find our lessons and our growth in that struggle."

Chedrick nodded his head. "I had wondered about that. I had a feeling…"

Davol interrupted. "I know. But this was the right time to tell you."

There was a silence.

"I have something else to tell you, boy.

The next time you come to this island of Avalon, you will help to change your world, but at this moment, dear Chedrick, YOUR world must change."

Knowing what was about to happen, both men had tears glistening in their eyes. One errant drop fell from Davol's eye and stained his light blue robe.

Davol stood, turned, and took a step away from Chedrick, toward the morning mist covering the still waters in front of them. He turned again for a few moments, looking back at the youth he had raised to be the finest of men. His blue eyes flashed and sparkled, while tears of mixed joy, pride, and farewell flowed freely, unchecked, down his ancient cheeks and wet the soil below.

He waved a silent farewell to Chedrick, turned, and walked out onto the water as though it were solid land, toward the barely visible distant shore. As he strolled purposely across the water, he dissolved forever from Chedrick's sight into the fabled mists of Avalon.

There was a strong blue glow in the depths of the mist as Davol faded completely from view. There was a resonant, deep-throated chortle that seem to come from everywhere and nowhere as the ancient scholar faded into nothingness.

A moment later, his voice came floating back over the water to Chedrick.

"... and you, my boy, ...are ME!"

EPILOGUE

Chedrick spent four days camping alone on the island, processing all that had happened, hoping against hope that Davol would return.

On the fifth day, Chedrick broke camp, packed everything up, and headed out into the world.

For over a decade, Chedrick wandered the countryside, performing tasks throughout the land and gaining more knowledge, ever-greater abilities, and a reputation known to all. Among the secrets taught to him by Davol was the secret of long life and robust good health for himself. Even though he was in his early thirties, he looked to the casual observer more like a tall, strapping youth of twenty.

One year, in late May, Chedrick found himself camping in the Vale of Mallerstang, by the river Eden. The sun was high in the sky, but not yet midday when four armed horsemen, accompanied by an empty–saddled horse, approached his camp, carrying an upright banner bearing the coat of arms of Uther Pendragon.

The leader of the group dismounted and approached Chedrick with an authoritative air.

"His highness, Uther Pendragon, requests your presence at his court."

The manner in which it was presented, and the looks on the men's faces, gave no doubt that this was far more than a simple request.

With a quiet smile, Chedrick began packing his meager belongings.

"I will. I shall be happy to oblige his Majesty."

Tying his bedroll behind the saddle, Chedrick mounted the horse, and the party set off toward the castle in nearby Cumbria.

While Uther Pendragon did not have a reputation as being a softhearted or compassionate king, he maintained among his servants, in fulfillment of a promise to his father, Constantine III, an aged and decrepit manservant named Galefridus.

Galefridus was not only old and slow-moving, he was profoundly deaf.

He also announced visitors to the king.

When Chedrick arrived at the castle, his escorts urged him through the doors, toward the throne room, where the king was holding court. The heavy oak doors, twice as tall as a man, were shut tightly, and a well-armed and very competent-looking guard stood in front of each one.

Standing ten feet in front of the doors, Galefridus intercepted the party, demanding to know who this stranger was that was being brought before the king.

This caused a bit of consternation. The proximity to the king forbade loud voices, and Galefridus was so deaf that he seldom got things right. He was also so old, that once he did get things right, he seldom remembered them that way.

After what seemed an eternity, Galefridus seemed to have gotten Chedrick's name and title correctly; "Chedrick the magician, Li'in of the Mers."

Unfortunately, in the three minutes between getting it, and the actual act of introducing Chedrick to the king, most of the information had slipped out of Galefridus' poor head. What was left came out as, simply, "Your Majesty, I present to you the magician, Mer Li'in."

And thus, he was introduced to Uther.

And thus, was born Merlin, the magician.

Uther retained Merlin for years and became his patron. In return, Merlin made Uther's castle a frequent stop on his journeys.

Years passed, and one dark night, Uther summoned Chedrick now Merlin to his chamber, and dismissed his guards.

The king silently beckoned Merlin to his side, and whispered in his ear, "Merlin, I would ask a favor of you..."

History has told the story of the birth of King Arthur a thousand times.

After Arthur was born, he was taken by Merlin to be raised by Sir Ector, who raised him with his own son, known later as Sir Kay.

Eventually, Merlin returned to the magical place called Avalon, to witness a young Arthur receiving a magical sword from an ethereal woman who rose from the sacred waters. The man who once was Chedrick, could have sworn that he heard a distant chortling as the young man took the sword in hand.

This is the end of this part of THIS story, but, as with EVERY ending, it is only another beginning in disguise.

There are many other stories yet to be told.

FINIS

When Merlin was 97 years old and nearing the end of his own life, he Traveled back for one last visit with Davol, to the old Atlan of Davol's time.

Davol is 887 years old.

He is sitting with his knees drawn up under his chin, hugging his shins, and staring out to sea from the spot where Robo had fallen to his death so many years before.

Merlin has brought his body along with him on this trip.

He appears silently, slightly behind Davol, who, without turning, pats the grass next to him as an invitation for Merlin to join him.

The two old friends sit in silence, staring out to sea until the sun begins to set.

No words are spoken between them, but their hearts communicate all that is necessary.

Davol's heart finally stops beating as he gazes into the setting sun reflected on the placid water, and he returns to the realm of Spirit, only to be reborn once more, at another time and place...

I wonder…

Is he, perhaps, YOU?